Recovery

NICOLE DYKES

❀ Created with Vellum

This book is dedicated to anyone who didn't receive the love they deserved from the very beginning. To all the forgotten children and victims of violence, don't lose your faith. There is still good out there, and you will find it.

Save A Place

1969

Behind These Hazel Eyes

Abandoning Sunday

Underdog

Alicia Keys

Hold Me While You Wait

Lewis Capaldi

Here

Alessia Cara

All These Things That I've Done

The Killers

Welcome To The Black Parade

My Chemical Romance

Home is Such A Lonely Place

Blink 182

One More Light

Linkin Park

I HAVEN'T SEEN Rhys for years, but it still feels the same being near him. Being in his embrace feels comforting somehow, like being held by a big brother. It brings me back to when I was nine years old and he was twelve. We were both skinny and dirty kids, but he told me on that day he'd look out for me.

Clearly I believed him.

The door dings, and when it opens, I hear, "Rhys?"

Rhys stiffens and lets me go, stepping back like he's surprised with himself. "Blair."

I turn to where he's looking and see a beautiful blond woman, the rich bitch type, eyeing me with uncertainty and then looking at him. "Are we adopting another kid?"

Kid? I'm twenty, not a kid. And what does she mean by "adopting"? I focus on Rhys and notice a rose gold band around his left ring finger. "You're married?"

He gives a quick nod, still clearly not someone with a ton of words. It's been so long since I've been around him. It's been so long since I've felt safe. "Yes. This is my wife, Blair." He turns toward her, and I swear I almost see a hint of a smile on his face.

That's new.

"And no. This one's over eighteen." He looks pained as he gazes at his beautiful wife. "She was like a little sister to me."

1

I feel the guilt flowing off him. Guilt of leaving us all behind. But I never blamed him. *Hell, who wouldn't get out if they got the chance?*

He was just out of high school and badly in need of rehab. I was back with my mother at the time. We hadn't exactly been around each other much when he left town anyway.

I see Christian hovering toward the back of the store, and it pains me to see him again too. I haven't seen him since Charity and I were seniors in high school. Since she took off. He looks different. More grown up. Less sad. And for whatever reason, that doesn't make me think he's okay. I sense it's fake, but I can barely feel anything at the moment.

Still numb and so agonizingly tired of everything.

"Tell me what happened to Trey," Rhys demands my attention, and I focus on him, my chest aching and my soul tired. I've just told him I'd come straight from Trey's funeral, blurting it out because how do you say that without it being a shock? Trey was a kid, and now he's gone forever.

"I can't." I shake my head from side to side in slow motion, trying to will away the memory of my little brother laying in the dirt outside our house.

He nods his head. "Okay."

"He's gone, Rhys. And I hate everything." My eyes lower to the floor. "Everyone."

Getting right to business, not prodding me any further for details, he asks, "Do you need somewhere to stay?" Still the same Rhys.

I lift my eyes to him. "Have you noticed how similar St. Louis and Kansas City are?" We grew up in Kansas City. In the worst part of Kansas City where, if you visit there, they tell you not to go. Where the sounds of ambulances, police chases, and gunshots are frequent. I shiver at the thought.

He seems to be thinking it over. "Yeah. They are. What can I do?" He sounds almost desperate to help me.

Nothing is going to truly help, but I feel like clawing at my own skin, trying to escape this hellish feeling. I don't want to be anywhere near that town.

I'm not sure why I tracked Rhys down. He's a few years older than me. We met in foster care when I was nine, one of the many times my mom messed up and lost us to the system. But unfortunately for us, she always got us back. Still, it's not like Rhys is the warm and cuddly type. Most people are probably afraid of him at first, all large, tattooed and usually wearing a scowl.

But for me, he always seemed like a safe haven, at least until he lost himself to the drugs. I have no one else in this world. Sean, Rhys's best friend and another big brother type to me, is in New York, and he sounded so damn happy on the phone. I couldn't run to him.

I couldn't pull him down.

I shouldn't be here, threatening to do the same thing to Rhys. "There's nothing you could do. I just . . ." I look over at my shoulder, seeing that his wife seems to be giving us some space. I look back to Rhys. "I don't know what to do."

"You're welcome to stay here, but I get the sense you don't want to."

I shake my head. "I need a change." But I barely have any money saved, especially after I bought the bus ticket to get here.

"How do you feel about Nashville?"

I quirk an eyebrow. "I have zero feelings about Nashville."

He nearly smiles again, which is just super weird for the guy I used to know. "Quinn is there with Logan. They're married and have a baby, but he has a shop, and she owns a bar there now. It's definitely a change."

Nashville? As in Tennessee?

"That's still a big city." *Noises. Cars. People. Violence.*

He nods. "I'll do anything I can to help you out. Just let me know what you need."

I was also close to Quinn for a little while. And now she's married to Logan? Last I knew, he disappeared on them all and went to live with his rich father who he'd never met, leaving them all behind. *He came back?*

I have no idea what's going on, and I feel tired and lightheaded. I don't know the last time I ate.

"If they have a new baby, they don't need me to worry about."

"You aren't an inconvenience. We look out for our own. Let me call them." He looks at me in question, and I nod my okay. He looks over at Blair, I think the two of them are having a silent conversation before he moves to the back of the shop.

Blair walks to my side. "You hungry?"

I turn toward her, still shocked Rhys is married. And to a Barbie type, although I think maybe this Barbie has claws. "Yes."

"Come on." She jerks her head toward the building across the street. It's a cute little bakery in a brick building.

I follow her without argument, too numb to fight. She buys me coffee and a pastry, and we sit down. "So, you were like Rhys's little sister? That must mean you're either Charity or Mya."

I lift an eyebrow and sip my coffee. "If he told you about me, then you know Charity is Christian's older sister." *Come on Barbie-with-an-Edge, use deduction.*

I have no idea how long Christian has worked for Rhys, but surely she knows a little about it. Probably picked up on him having pasty white skin and me *not* being white.

For Rhys to marry her, she must have some brains.

"Hey, I don't know if maybe you guys have different moms or dads." She smirks into her own coffee. "I never assume."

Huh. Maybe I do like her. "I'm Mya."

She nods her head. "And you're in some kind of trouble?"

I don't know her. I know Rhys married her, but I have no idea who he is anymore. Not really. All I know is the stupid-ass code we all had growing up, one that said we'd take care of our own. But let's be honest, it's only a code if you adhere to it. And some didn't.

Logan left.

Rhys left for rehab.

I haven't talked to Charity or Christian in two years. It seems most of us didn't keep our word. But it does seem like Rhys and Sean talk. And Quinn and Rhys. So, who the hell knows?

"No trouble."

She's studying me. "Rhys seemed worried." She doesn't ask me about Trey, and I'm grateful. I don't want to talk about my little brother.

Eleven. He was eleven years old.

So much blood. He was lifeless in my arms.

My stomach churns, and I look across the street, seeing Rhys out the front door. "Looks like your husband's looking for us."

She smiles at that and stands from her seat, and I follow, grabbing my coffee and what's left of my pastry. We cross the street, and Rhys addresses me, "I can get you on a flight tonight if that's what you want. They'll be happy to help." His eyes stay on mine. "But so will I."

I look around the crowded city street where his shop is located and shiver, listening to all the cars and noise. But Nashville won't be any different.

Still . . . it's further away.

"Okay," I choke out, "I can pay you back."

He waves me off. "Don't. Just . . ." He looks up at the sky, looking like he wants to scream, and I know the feeling. "I'm sorry about Trey." His gaze lowers to meet mine. "I'm so sorry."

I can feel he somehow feels responsible, which is a little egotistical considering we aren't blood-related and we hadn't seen him in years, but it's still so Rhys. "It's not your fault."

He doesn't believe me. "You want a flight out tomorrow instead? You can rest."

I nearly laugh at the thought. I haven't rested in a long, long time. And I doubt it's going to happen any time soon. "I need to go." I look back over my shoulder at Blair, who's standing there patiently, and then I look back at Rhys. "It seems like you have a really good life here, Rhys."

He shrugs his shoulders. "It's not so bad these days."

I nod my head, happy for him, wondering how he got here but

not enough to dig into the details. Not now anyway. "Thank you for your help."

"I know I left without any explanation, and when I got back—"

"Stop." I hold up a hand. "I wasn't waiting around for you to come back and save me, Rhys. We all wanted to help each other, but I think we all also knew we were on our own too."

I watch his throat bob with remorse and shake my head at him, not wanting it, not needing him to feel bad for leaving.

"Let's go."

I say a quick goodbye to Blair and wonder about Christian. But Rhys booked a quick flight, and we have to hurry. He wasn't joking about helping me out however he can. I only have one suitcase with me, small enough to carry on, and before I know it, I'm Nashville bound.

Far away from Kansas City, and hopefully I can escape all the memories there.

"LOGAN, WE HAVE A PROBLEM." Quinn walks through the front door, coming in hot as usual. Quinn is kind of a no-nonsense chick, straight to the point and not fucking around.

I like it.

She has her newborn in a sling against her body as Logan, my friend and employer, looks up from the tattoo he's currently working on—some middle age accountant-type going through a midlife crisis. "What's wrong?"

He looks at his kid, snuggled up to her chest, and then to Quinn with a questioning glance. I just started working on a piece of my own, only my customer is cuter—a blond with big tits and totally my type, but admittedly, most women are.

Finn, my best friend since we were little kids, is working on a different customer, and James has a customer of his own as well. We're usually pretty goddamn busy around here, and I'm not complaining, but still, all four of us have our eyes glued to Quinn.

We've made our own family here at Lyrics and Ink, Logan's tattoo shop, and anyone of us would lay our lives down for each other, but especially Quinn.

"Mya," she breathes, and now I'm even more intrigued. A chick's in trouble.

"I can help," I automatically volunteer.

Logan shoots me a sharp look that says no. "She's a kid."

"She's twenty, Logan," Quinn interjects, and I smile, going back to the tattoo on the blond's hip.

"Not a kid." I wink at the chick in my chair, and she giggles.

"She's a kid to me," Logan growls. "She was like . . ." he thinks about it, looking at Quinn, "ten the last time I saw her?"

She gives a quick nod. "Yeah, about that, I think."

I have no idea who the fuck they're talking about, but they grew up together in Kansas City. Finn and I grew up in small-town Kansas, but we all moved down here. And I, for one, haven't looked back since.

"What's wrong?" Logan asks again.

Quinn looks sick and is quiet, pulling all our attention to her again as tears well up in her eyes. "Trey died."

"What the fuck are you talking about?" Logan looks horrified, and I wonder who Trey is.

"Who's that?" Finn asks.

Her breath is shaky. "Her little brother."

"Jesus." Logan sweeps his hand over his face in distress. "He was what? Eleven?"

She nods. What? Eleven? That's so fucking young.

She seems to hold her baby a little closer, and you can't blame her when we're talking about this.

"What happened?" Logan asks, not touching his customer anymore.

She shakes her head. "I don't know. Rhys didn't ask."

"Of course he didn't," Logan muses, his hand shaking with nerves or shock from the news.

"I can finish up if you need to go." I nod at his hand, trying not to make it too obvious.

He shakes his hand out and inhales deeply before letting it go. "No." He looks to Quinn. "Unless you need me to?"

She shakes her head at him quickly. "She's coming here. Her flight will be in soon. I'll pick her up."

"She's coming here?" Logan sounds surprised.

Quinn nods. "She had to get out of there."

He accepts that. "Do you want me to pick her up?" He looks down at his client. "I can cancel the rest of my appointments."

She waves him off. "I'm capable." She turns to James. "That is, if your husband can handle the bar?"

James merely smirks. "I wouldn't leave him in charge of shit."

He sounds nonchalant, but I've never seen a couple more fiercely protective than James and Tommy. Then I look over at Quinn. Okay, maybe Quinn and Logan. But still.

She rolls her eyes. "Whatever. I'm going to go tell him." She shoots me a look. "Hands-off."

I hold my hands up in surrender, still holding onto my tattoo gun. "What?"

She doesn't even bother with a further warning before leaving, and I turn to Logan. "Thanks for the backup, buddy. As if I would hurt your friend."

He chuckles and shakes his hand again, calming his nerves and going back to work. "She'll always be a ten-year-old kid to me. Don't touch her."

His middle-aged client smirks over at me, and I shake my head, choosing to look at my client instead. She has a better rack. "Can you believe this shit?"

She laughs at that, pushing her tits up in her tank top. "No. You seem perfectly innocent to me."

I don't tire of that accent. Sweetly southern. And although she's only twenty-one—I checked her ID—sounds like she's had a diet composed of only whiskey and cigarettes for half her life. "I'm an angel."

I wink again, and Logan scoffs, "Stop hitting on the clients."

"What? You think you're my boss or something?" I shoot back. He just shakes his head.

"I like it," the girl drawls, wetting her lips with her tongue. I could probably have a night with this chick, but I'm growing tired of that shit.

I should probably ask Logan more questions about this Mya chick, but I figure he'll tell me what he wants me to know.

I'm not really one to pry.

And it sounds like I'll be meeting her soon enough anyway.

It's past ten when my plane touches down in Nashville. I discover Quinn waiting to pick me up at the airport. I'm worn and still numb, not allowing my mind to go to Trey the entire flight even if that's where it relentlessly tried to go.

I just stayed frozen.

Quinn looks almost the same as the last time I saw her, which wasn't that long ago. But it feels like a lifetime has passed. She still dresses the same, jeans and an oversized tee swallowing her frame, although now she has a glistening wedding ring on her finger and a baby strapped to her chest.

Holy. Shit.

It's insane how much can change in a few years.

"Hi, Mya." Her voice is still sweet and raspy, her blue eyes filled with unshed tears.

"Hi, Quinn."

We go out to her car, and after she secures her infant in the back, we drive the streets of Nashville. It's all lit up, bright from neon as she navigates through the city, deep into the heart. I cringe at all the cars around us. It's definitely a big city, and I crave desolate land, a whole lot of nothing. But at least it's not Kansas City.

She doesn't ask about Trey or what happened. It's not really her style to pry. She parks her car in front of a building tucked in with several other shops and businesses. I see "Lyrics and Ink" printed on the large glass window, and I smile.

Quinn has always loved music. It's something we used to have in common. She taught me a lot about pitch and different notes when I was a kid, eager to learn with hope in my heart. Hope that I might get out of where we came from and find my way to a stage.

Stupid.

She points to the building next to the one we're parked in front of. "So, that's the bar, the Lyrics part of Lyrics and Ink." I notice that door has the same symbol as the tattoo shop. "And then . . ." she points to the other door, "that's the tattoo parlor. The Ink. We can put you to work at either place."

"I don't know how to tattoo anyone," I try to joke, but my tone comes out dull and flat.

"They could use a receptionist." She looks over to the bar. "But I'm partial to the Lyrics side." She cocks her head to the side. "You still sing?"

I shake my head quickly, shutting that shit down. "No."

She studies me but then shrugs it off easily. "Okay. We can always use a waitress. Completely up to you."

I shouldn't be surprised they're so willing to help, but it's still hard to accept. Although I did go to Rhys. I had no other choice.

"I definitely have waitress experience." My eyes meet hers, and I hope I've softened my gaze. "Thank you, Quinn."

"Don't sweat it. You can stay with Logan and me if you want to." She looks into the backseat. "But it does get a little noisy in the night."

I smile at that, looking back at her sleeping baby.

"Or you can stay in the loft above." She points up, and I look up at the brick space above the shop with a few windows.

"That would be great. I'll pay rent."

She waves me off and turns off the car, opening her door. "Don't worry about it. You'll have a few roommates though."

My entire body tenses, but I don't object. I can't. I just need to be patient and save. Then I'll get far away from humans.

"Okay. That's fine." I hop out and grab my bag as she grabs her baby. We go into the tattoo parlor, and I see Logan immediately. He seems to be the only one here.

"Mya." He stands up. "Holy shit. You grew up."

Quinn rolls her eyes. "Men." She hands their baby to him, and he cradles the still sleeping infant to his chest. She smiles at him, and I see the same love they've always had for each other in her eyes. "She's going to live upstairs with the guys."

His brows furrow. "You sure that's a good idea?"

"It's fine," I cut in, the exhaustion growing to be too much.

He grins, a playful smirk on his face, and he seems happy. "Well, you better give them hell then."

I have no idea who "the guys" are or why he's smirking, but I don't care. "That's pretty much what I do."

He smiles and then sadness comes over him. I know he wants to say something about Trey, but he doesn't. Quinn leads me up the stairs at the back of the shop and then pushes open a metal door that looks heavy.

"Jesus fuck, Quinn." We walk in, and a guy—a fucking hulk of a man, all muscles and tattoos—puts his hand over his heart like we startled him. I notice instantly he's dressed only in a white towel. His muscles are pulled tight and tense, inked ridges and lines. I struggle to look up at his face. He grins at me, his teeth straight and white. His facial hair is scruffy but not a full beard. "Who's your friend?"

Quinn is not amused as she folds her arms over her chest. "She's your new roommate, so you better put on some fucking clothes."

"You kiss my friend with that mouth?" He wiggles his eyebrows at her, and if I were in a better mood, or in a better life, maybe I would find him charming as hell.

"I do a lot more than that." Quinn winks, and he chuckles as he hold out his large hand for mine.

I notice the full sleeve of tattoos on that arm, the other only has a couple. His chest isn't covered in them, but he has a few there too. "I'm Jase."

13

"Mya," I say, not taking his hand. I don't want to touch him. I don't want anyone touching me.

He shrugs it off and drops his hand just as another man comes up to us, wrapping an arm around him. If I thought Jase was huge, this guy is fucking massive. Jesus. What the hell do they feed them down here?

This one has sandy brown hair as opposed to the black hair Jase has on his head. Jase's hair is wet, but a little shorter than this one's. And this guy is dressed in a black hoodie and jeans. "You got us a girl roommate, Quinn?" He's eyeing me like a wolf but sporting a bright smile that seems friendly.

"She's not for either of you fuckers."

"Well, she sure isn't for Tommy or James," Jase says, dragging his fingers through his hair, and I'm ashamed of myself when my eyes track the muscles of his bicep and forearm flexing tightly.

More men? Jesus.

Quinn rolls her eyes at him again. "Not. For. You." Her tone is direct, like a big sister's, and it's oddly comforting even though I should be annoyed. I don't need anyone looking out for me.

The guy nods his head at me, his gaze trailing down my body before meeting my eyes. "Well, that's a damn shame."

"Ignore him," Quinn says.

"Don't ignore me, sweetheart. That would break my heart." The guy feigns hurt, and I roll my eyes, but he just continues to smile. "I'm Finn."

"Mya," I say again. I turn to Quinn. "Who are Tommy and James?"

She looks around the empty loft and then looks at Finn. "Where are they?"

"Probably fucking." He points with his thumb behind him.

And Jase nods his head, his bottom lip protruding. "More than likely. They headed to their room like ten minutes ago."

Quinn nods her head. "They're married and live in that room." She points to where Finn was just gesturing.

A little relief goes through me. Two less men trying to get into my pants. I look at Jase and Finn, no trace of a smile on my face.

It's okay. They can try.

They'll learn real fucking quick, I'm not here to play.

Good. God. What the fuck was Quinn thinking? She just brought the most beautiful girl I've ever seen into our loft, said she's living here now, and expects me not to make a move.

I mean holy fuck.

I'm not sure who she thinks I am, but I'm not *that* fucking guy.

This girl just got off a flight and still . . . gorgeous. Her black hair is down and curly, a beautiful fucking wild mane I want to feel between my fingers with a sexy golden hue to it. Her big brown eyes have golden flecks in them to match. Her lips are full and red. Her skin is a flawless deep caramel color that looks so goddamn silky and smooth.

She's tall for a chick but would still only come up to about my shoulders. Her body is lithe, and I'd say she's a runner but still has fucking fine curves. Her lips form a straight line, giving off an "I will cut you" vibe, but I don't fucking care. I can take some pain.

Probably more than most.

Seriously, what was Quinn thinking?

Of course, I do have to remind myself she just went through a tragedy, and I'm not a total prick, so I pull it back a little.

Quinn pushes past Finn, eyeing me. "Get dressed." Mya follows behind her as Quinn leads her to the one empty bedroom in the loft, the one next to mine.

I don't follow Quinn's order to get dressed, and I smirk over at Finn, who looks like he wants to pounce.

We never fight over women. Never. It's a code with us.

But I think I might go toe-to-toe with the huge motherfucker for this girl.

"Thank you, Quinn." I hear her sultry voice, quiet with exhaustion. "Really. Thank you."

Quinn gives a quick nod. "It's no problem." Her eyes narrow on Finn and me across the room. "If they give you any trouble, let me know."

Mya gives a small smile and a nod of her own head. "I'll be fine."

I grin at that, having no doubt. Pretty sure if anyone's in trouble here, it's me. Quinn leaves her there, walking toward us, her don't-fuck-with-me look perfected. "She better be fine."

We both nod our heads in agreement, but it's me that pokes the angry mama bear. "Don't worry. I'll take the best care of her."

She punches me in the arm, and I laugh, rubbing the spot because she has bony fucking fingers. "Jase. I love you like a brother, but I will kill you."

I laugh at that, knowing it's true. "I'll be good."

She looks over at Finn, who raises his hands in surrender. "Me too."

"Good." She pushes past us again and heads out the door. Finn closes it behind her, and Mya disappears into her room without another word. Maybe she's tired. Or maybe she didn't want the awkward small talk.

I can appreciate both, but what kind of roommate would I be if I didn't try to get to know her a little?

Finn clearly has the same idea and is already heading to her room.

Motherfucker.

I follow him, still only in a towel, but there's no time to dress. We both reach her open door at the same time, and I see she's looking around the room. It's pretty bare. Just a bed, a side table, and a dresser at the moment.

"Do you need anything?" I ask.

She turns around to look at us, clearly not happy to see us from the look on her pretty face. "No. I'm fine."

"You sure?" Finn prods, and I feel my body tense with irritation.

"I'm sure." Her big brown eyes meet mine. "I just need sleep."

I don't miss her eyes trailing over my chest, and I can't hide my grin. My body doesn't offer sleep, but she's sure looking at it.

She drags her eyes back up to my face and then looks over at Finn. "Can I help you guys with something?"

Attitude is dripping from her, and it does nothing to suppress my need to get to know her. She lost her little brother. She left her home to come here.

Suddenly and without warning, it hits me hard that beyond the deep brown orbs with golden flecks, there's agony. Grief. Guilt. Regret. Deep-seated pain that more than likely goes deeper than losing her brother. I see other shit besides her body and the beautiful face glaring over at my best friend and me. I see anguish.

Fuck.

My throat dries, and I feel like a dick as I take a step back. "We'll let you get some rest then."

Finn looks over at me as I nudge him in the side and jerk my head toward the living room. He huffs reluctantly, "Yeah. We'll see ya tomorrow. Hopefully you like eggs. I'm fucking great at making eggs."

I roll my eyes, but he's rewarded with a small smile that makes my chest ache, already wanting to see that again. "Thanks."

We leave, and I pull her door shut to give her privacy, walking into my room next to hers and sensing Finn follow me in. "Dibs."

I grab a shirt and pull it on. "No."

"Bullshit. No. That's how this works."

I grab some jeans and tug them on before ripping off my towel. "No," I say again, not entertaining his claim on her for even a second.

"What the fuck, man?" He sits down on my bed.

"She's our roommate, dipshit." And she's mine. I don't say it

19

though. Especially because it sounds fucking stupid and caveman-esque. "Quinn and Logan aren't going to like us slobbering all over her."

"Pretty sure I saw your drool on the floor out there, asshole."

I shrug my shoulders. "Let's go to the bar. Blow off some steam."

"Whatever," he huffs, and I know he's not really that into her. I know my best friend well, and she'd just be a plaything to him till he got bored.

He won't fight me for her.

Good.

I WAKE up the next morning, still tired. Still numb. I'm starting to think this is just how my life is going to be from now on—haunting nightmares, sickening abyss, not caring, not awake even when my eyes are open, just floating through life and hating everything.

I climb out of the bed that was surprisingly comfortable and stretch my arms to the sky. I'm only wearing a thin t-shirt, but it's large and goes almost to my knees. After ducking into the bathroom, I slowly make my way toward the kitchen area of the loft, praying they have coffee.

I hear booming male voices before I reach them and see four men all crowded in the kitchen. Jase is the first I see, and he's dressed today, wearing tight black jeans that have holes in them with a gray hoodie that clings to his body.

A body I've already seen far too much of and shamelessly checked out almost every inch of. I blame the exhaustion and grief.

Finn turns to me, his dark blue eyes shining as he nods to me. "Ah, our new roommate's up! Fucking finally. You think I was going to make breakfast for just these fuckers?"

I notice he has a spatula in his hand and is, in fact, making eggs in the frying pan on the stove. "I really just need coffee," I say, and I know it's rude. I know they want to be friendly, but I just want to be invisible.

"Coffee is much better than the shitty eggs Finn makes," one of the two men I haven't yet met says as he walks to the coffee pot and pours a cup before handing it to me. "I'm Tommy."

I stare at him, and then my eyes go to the man sitting at the island bar in the kitchen. That must be his husband, James, and I wasn't fucking kidding about what they feed them down here. All four men are massive and tattooed. James is Black like me with his hair trimmed short and a bright white smile.

Tommy is Hispanic, I think. He has the same rich bronze tone my friend Veronica has.

All four of them are broad and thick with muscle. All gorgeous, with bright, shiny smiles and tattoos. If I was a normal girl, I'd be in heaven right now.

"I'm Mya. I . . ." I look around again and then back to Tommy. I take the coffee mug from him. "I won't be here long."

He just smiles at that, shaking his head and taking a seat next to his husband. "Yeah. I said that too."

James looks to me. "Yeah. I think we all thought we wouldn't be here long." He looks over at Jase and Finn who are on the other side of the island. "But they aren't so bad."

Jase raises his middle finger, and I see it too is tattooed. "Fuck off, we're great." His voice is deep and smooth. And his eyes are a beautiful hazel color. I notice this as they lock on me. "You sleep okay?"

I nod my head, taking a drink of coffee. He seems a little different today. Less playful. Less flirty. I'm not sure I like it. He's looking at me like a wounded bird, someone who needs to be treated with care.

"Fine."

Finn fills a plate with eggs and bacon and places it on the bar. "Eat."

It's an order. I haven't been told what to do for a long time. As if he knows it's a mistake to boss me around, Jase leans his ass back against the counter, hot mug of coffee in his hands which he brings up to his mouth with a smirk, still eyeing me.

"No thanks," I say, holding up the coffee. "I just need a caffeine fix."

"You start work with me today," Tommy says, sliding the plate closer to the edge toward me. "Eat and then I'll show you the ropes."

Are they for real?

"No. Thanks." I look at Tommy, assuming he must work at the bar. "I'm going to get ready, and then I'll be there."

Finn places a hand over his heart like he did last night, like he's wounded. "I slaved over the stove for you and you aren't even going to take a bite?"

"Don't do it," James coughs into his hand. They all laugh and joke around. I sneak out, going to the bathroom to take a shower. When I turn off the water, I grab a fresh towel from the linen closet in the bathroom, surprised that four men have managed to do laundry themselves. But this place is fairly tidy.

I wrap the towel around myself, tucking the corner of it between my breasts and looking outside the door before darting into my room and getting dressed.

When I'm finished getting ready, I walk out toward the living room and kitchen. I only see Jase now. The place is empty and quiet, his large body sitting comfortably in a chair in the living room with a plate in front of him on the coffee table.

"You can eat now. No one else is here."

I huff, annoyed, and my brows press together. "You think I care about people watching me eat?"

His large shoulders shrug in indifference. "I know you didn't want to eat, but you have to be starving." His hazel eyes lift up to look at mine. "We live together. We'll probably be sharing some meals."

"No. We won't."

"Is that so?" His tone is light, playful, but his voice is gravely and sexy. I hate it. Because I don't.

"Yes. I'm not here for some fun, little sitcom-type comedy. I'm here to earn money and get the hell out."

"Out of what?"

I freeze, not liking that I've already said more than I intend. "Just out. I'm going down to the bar."

"You should eat." It's matter-of-fact and annoying.

"Why the hell do you all care? You don't even know me."

"We would know you if you would calm the fuck down and just talk to us. Tell us more than your name and that you crave coffee."

I stare at him, annoyed and frustrated. That's not an option. I don't want to know them. "No."

He just stares me down, unafraid to piss me off, which is infuriating. "No? Just no."

"Yes. No."

He grins playfully and picks up the plate, poking the pieces of scrambled eggs with his fork and bringing it to his full lips. "Last chance?"

My stomach grumbles at the sight, but pride is one thing I have an abundance of. "Go for it."

He opens his mouth and takes a bite of the eggs, moaning exaggeratedly, and my stomach flutters at the strong male sound, which is primal and sexy like he wants so much more than eggs. He's too good-looking. Too sexy. Too everything. I bail as quickly as I can, making my way to the door and jerking it open, going down the stairs and into the tattoo parlor.

Logan is the first person I see. "Hey. You okay?"

No. That man up there is all sorts of temptation. And that is the last thing I need.

"I'm fine. Is the only way into the bar from outside?"

I'm not sure he believes I'm fine, but luckily he guides me to the back room, I think it must be where they relax if they get a break, but the shop is already full this morning. "This is the employee entrance."

He pushes open a door leading into the kitchen of the bar. "Thanks."

He nods. "Tommy's in there already."

I walk through a swinging door and look around at the bar. It's small. A hole-in-the-wall really, but I like it. It has a certain charm to it. Wooden booths and a few tables. A wooden bar with whiskey posters surrounding it. And a stage.

A beautiful, small stage with a single microphone up front. I swallow the pain burning up from my belly. The ache I have to stand on that stage and belt out musical notes, to get lost for a moment in the light and music, is too great.

"You sing?"

I look over at Tommy who's standing behind the bar.

"No."

His brow furrows, and I know he doesn't believe me. But I don't care. I'm not here to get to know anyone.

He shows me the ropes, tells me the basic schedule. It's nothing out of the ordinary. I wasn't lying when I said I have waitressing experience. My first fake ID wasn't to buy alcohol, it was to get a job as a waitress when I was thirteen. They knew I wasn't sixteen yet, but they paid under the table, and it worked out for us both. Seedy and shady, that's my life.

They don't open until eleven, and Tommy tells me I'll be on the night shift with him for the rest of the week. However today, we're both taking the easier day shift.

I thank him, and before we open, he cooks us both hamburgers and delicious greasy fries I can't say no to.

We sit in the booth and eat in silence. I feel oddly comfortable with him. He doesn't put my body on full alert the way Jase does. None of them do.

For whatever reason, Jase is dangerous to me.

I'm DONE with my shift at Lyrics and Ink and want nothing more than to go to the bar and check on Mya. But I know that's not a good idea.

I'm not sure what it is about this chick, but I couldn't stop thinking about her today. The stubbornness in her. To some people, she may seem cold, but not to me. I see her. I see the pain she wants to hide, that she wants to smash so far down no one can call her on it. She wants to make herself as small as possible so no one will pay attention to her.

But that's impossible.

Instead of going to the bar, I go upstairs, but she's not at the bar. She's in the living room and on the couch with Tommy.

"What are you doing here?" I direct my question at Tommy who looks up from the mindless television they're watching, something on MTV.

"We took the morning shift. Thought she might need some time to ease into it, but I was wrong." He winks at Mya. "She's a pro."

Mya's mouth lifts into a small smile before she wipes it away and stands up. "I'm going to my room."

I want to beg her to stay, dig deeper into who she is. But of course, I know that wouldn't work with her. She leaves, and I plop down next to Tommy. "Pro, huh?"

He smiles. "She's amazing. Handles customers well. Even knows how to work for tips."

I feel a growl bubbling up in my throat at the thought. "What the fuck does that mean?"

He eyes me with suspicion. "Aw, do you have a little crush?"

"Fuck off."

He, of course, does not fuck off. He laughs, and if I didn't love him like a brother, I'd punch him for it. I met Tommy and James when I moved here with Finn, but we all clicked right away, formed a bond. And even though James and Tommy were a well-established couple by then, we all moved in here together. I don't think any of us have plans to move out any time soon.

It just works.

But now, Mya's here, and everything feels a little off-kilter. I want to know why she's so closed off. Why she's so determined not to get to know us. Why she wants out. Where the fuck is out?

She just left Kansas City.

Instead, I just go to my room and lay on my bed, looking up at the shelf full of trophies. I close my eyes and hear the crowd roaring loudly, my teammates out on the field, the crack of helmets, the smell of the mud and earth.

It feels like only minutes later, but when I open my eyes, I see how dark it is outside and know I must have been out for a while. I climb out of bed and see the loft is dark. It's also quiet, so I'm assuming Finn is still at work.

I go into the kitchen, flicking on the light. My stomach is grumbling, and I decide to make some tacos, knowing we'll eat the leftovers tomorrow. When the meat is sizzling in the pan, I look over to see Mya walking into the kitchen.

She's wearing the same thing she was this morning after her shower. A thin striped tee with a wide neck and little jean shorts. She's beautiful with no effort. Her hair is down, the curls so fucking sexy.

"Hungry?" I ask, at this point not even expecting an audible reply.

She nods her head and walks to the fridge. "I bought some things earlier."

She pulls out some lunchmeat and closes the door, grabbing a loaf of bread from the counter. "A sandwich?" I raise an eyebrow.

"Nothing wrong with a sandwich for dinner." She grabs two pieces of bread and keeps her head down.

I don't like it, how her head is tilted down looking away, trying to disappear.

"There is when there are tacos."

"I don't want anything from you."

The comment stings, and I'm not sure why. "From me?"

She looks over at me, her voice not hiding how tired she is. "From anyone."

Pride. I get it.

I also don't say it. I don't want to kick her down even if I want to challenge her. Now just doesn't seem like the right time to do that.

"Okay."

"That's it?" She's gaping at me, those brown eyes showing her curiosity.

"What do you mean?" I turn off the burner and move the skillet back.

"No more questions? No trying to get me to eat tacos?"

I grin slyly at her. "Why? You want some?"

She looks away again, fastening the bread package closed and putting her sandwich together. "No."

There's that word again.

"You know, eventually, when a human being gets turned down enough, they stop trying."

She freezes and then turns her body to face me. "I wouldn't know."

"Never been rejected?" That I can imagine.

"Never had anyone try." Now I'm the one who's curious as she turns away, grabbing her sandwich and fading away down the hall.

Wanting to dissipate into thin air.

I know that feeling.

I know it well.

I sit straight up in bed, my heart racing and my breathing rapid. Another loud crack and my bedroom is lit up with lightening, the rain pelting the window.

Jesus.

I've only been here for a week, and Nashville has been pounded with thunderstorms for three days of it. I'm not afraid of storms, but it pulled me from my deep sleep, and my body is on full alert now.

I decide to get up, maybe grab a drink of water. When I walk out of my room, I brush against a hard body. Bare flesh. I look up at the figure in the dark and see Jase through the small amount of light streaming in from the streetlights outside. He's only wearing a pair of boxers, with his hair all tousled and messy.

He must have been asleep too.

"Fuck! What time is it?"

I shake my head. "I didn't check."

I hear muffled sounds coming from the bedroom across from mine and then the sounds grow louder and are distinctly feminine.

Jase shakes his head. "Guess Finn found someone tonight."

I saw him at the bar during my shift tonight. If I had to guess, it's the busty redhead who was all over him when I clocked out. "Guess so."

31

"You okay?" He yawns slightly, using his hand to cover his mouth. "You aren't afraid of storms, are you?"

I nearly laugh at that. If only I were afraid of something like that. No, my fears run much deeper. "No. I'm not. But it's loud."

He agrees in a nod. "Well, you're welcome to hang out in my room til it passes."

"Are you afraid of storms?" I question, eyeing him, maybe a little lilt in my voice that I didn't pull back in time.

He grins. "Yeah. You wanna hold me?"

I roll my eyes. There's that flirtatious asshole he was the first night. "Hold yourself."

He laughs at that. "Come on. I'm not so bad."

That's what I'm afraid of. Lightning crackles outside, and I sigh, lifting my shoulders. "Fine."

He looks surprised but then leads me into his room. I look around at the room that has the same layout as mine. Bed, table and a dresser. He has a small flat screen television on his dresser though. He leaves the door open, and I take a seat on the edge of his bed.

He sits at a respectful distance, and I'm appreciative.

This is stupid. What are we going to do? I look at his bed, the covers are pushed down and haphazard, so I'm pretty sure he was just sleeping here, and I try not to think about all of the things we could do there.

It's been a while since I've been touched by anyone. And I don't want to give in to the inherent carnal need for human contact. I want to believe I'll be just fine without that.

"So, how's work going?" His smile is friendly, but I don't think Jase is all that friendly. I don't think he'd hurt me on purpose either.

"Oh, so that's the small talk we're going for? Work?"

He chuckles and lays back on his bed, looking up at the ceiling, and I try not to look at his body stretched out on the bed. I try to ignore how much space his large, muscular form takes up on the bed. "At least I tried."

He's always trying. I don't know this man. We met a week ago. But still . . . it feels like he wants me to be okay. He wants me to eat.

He wants to ask how I like work. He tries, puts so much effort into everything, and I hate it.

I don't want to be worn down and give in to his charm. I want to keep my head down and just be, just barely exist at the bare minimum until I get far away from other people. Until I can just not care anymore.

Because caring leads to pain, and I've had enough of that to last a lifetime.

"What's going on in that head?" He's gazing up at me, and I have the urge to tuck myself next to him and then bury my head in next and escape that way.

I look away from him and up to a shelf on the wall, a shelf with a shitload of trophies. Holy. Shit.

"What the hell? Are you a champion of something?" I look closer. "Football?"

Huh. Makes sense with his build, I guess. I look down at his handsome face to see that his expression has darkened. "No."

That's my line.

"No, you never played football? Whose trophies are those?"

It's dark, and I can't make out the writing on them.

He sits up, clearing his throat. "Doesn't matter."

I could have sworn this man was an open book, someone with nothing to hide. But as I look into his eyes now, I see I definitely misjudged him. "You must have been good. That's a lot of trophies."

He shakes his head and shrugs his shoulders, and I recognize the look in his eyes. He's pleading with me to drop it. "I'm good at a lot of things."

His deep voice, husky and full of gravel makes that sentence extremely sexual. The fiery look in his eyes only adds to that. He looks like he wants to kiss me, and God, I want him to. I take a deep breath just as his lips meet mine.

I shouldn't let this happen.

This is far too close. What the hell am I doing?

I'm about to push him away, but I feel his hand on my hip, strong and sure. And then his tongue sweeps into my mouth. And damn it,

I just turn myself over to the moment. Because it's been so long since I've kissed anyone, since I've felt kind hands on me. So I lean into him. My cold hand pushes against the warm skin on his chest, feeling only the hard muscle.

We kiss with intensity and heat that I don't stop to question. I'm not sure my body has ever been this ready to be touched by another person. I kiss him deeper, starting to push him back onto the bed, but I feel his large hand move over mine, both resting on his chest. He pulls back. "Mya." He sounds breathless as I look at him in a daze.

"What's wrong?"

He looks like he's searching for the right words. "I umm . . ." I don't want to think. I want him to kiss me, but he doesn't. "I could barely get you to like me this last week. I've gotten maybe a few words from you, and now you're kissing me like maybe you want more to happen."

"So go with it," I whisper. I mean, he kissed me. Did he think I would push him away? Probably.

"I don't want to be your mistake."

"You've never had a one-night stand before?" I question, pretty sure I already know the answer.

"I have. A couple of times, but you're not that. At the very least, you're my roommate."

I roll my eyes in a huff, frustrated and not even sure why. I don't want anyone touching me. Maybe I should remind myself of that. I don't want to get close to anyone. "So, you're saying you wouldn't respect me in the morning?"

I try a joke, and it doesn't land. Maybe I need to stop with the jokes.

"You don't need my respect for validation, and if I thought this is really what you wanted, I wouldn't fucking hesitate."

I'm so angry I could scream because that's the most perfect thing any man has ever said to me. My eyes fill with tears, and I hate him for it. He pulls me into him and tucks my head to his chest. Tears stream down my face onto his skin, but he just holds me to him.

He moves us so our heads are on the pillows and our bodies under his covers, but he doesn't stop holding me. His much larger body holds mine so my face is against his chest, wrapped in his arms, and I just cry.

I just let it out, and I don't worry about the consequences. I weep into the arms of this man who is practically a stranger to me, and he lets me. It's a whole new kind of escape for me, one I wouldn't normally let myself do, but I need it.

For once, I give in.

Just for tonight.

Oh, fuck. She's in my bed. Mya is still curled up to my body, both of us still under the covers. Me only in boxers, her in that fucking thin t-shirt.

She looks peaceful as she sleeps, but I know she's probably anything but. I kissed her. I fucked up and kissed her. I know it was a mistake and not because she's a vulnerable woman who can't take care of herself.

Exactly the opposite.

She's strong and confident. *Fucking amazing.* And if anyone was vulnerable last night, at least before I kissed her, it was me. Fucking football trophies. I need to put them away, maybe throw them away. But for whatever reason, I leave them there to stare back at me. Remind me.

Mya stirs next to me, her large, beautiful eyes gazing up at me, looking slightly confused, maybe a little embarrassed. "I fell asleep?"

She did. After she started to sob in my chest and I held her, just letting her finally express some of the emotion inside her, the crying stopped slowly, and soon I could hear her breathing even out, lost in deep sleep. And then, I held her to me and closed my own eyes, drifting away.

"Yeah."

"I slept with you all night?" She looks freaked the fuck out.

I smile, my lips pulling up as I shrug my shoulder. "Don't worry, you only snored a little."

She rolls her eyes at me, but I see her lips lifting. "I don't snore."

I know she's not happy about letting her guard down, and I understand that. But I don't want her to regret it. "You're definitely a bed hog."

She sits up, using a band she has around her wrist to secure her curls into a ponytail. But then she groans, "God, they're going to think we slept together."

I sit up, stretching my arms into the air and giving her a pointed look. "Who the fuck cares? We aren't in high school."

"They're my roommates. I don't want them . . ."

"What?" I laugh. "Thinking you're easy. Trust me, none of us think that."

She tosses the pillow that was under her head moments ago at me, and it hits me in the chest. "I'll just have to tell them you turned me down."

I fight a groan because it wasn't easy, feeling her hand on my bare chest trying to nudge me backward. *What would her body have felt like on top of mine?* I'm pretty sure I know the answer to that. "And like I told you last night, if I thought you actually wanted it, I would have gone through with it, no problem."

"So, instead you just let me cry like a baby?"

She hates that she let her guard down. I sweep my thumb over her bottom lip that's so pouty and biteable, "I think you cried like a grown woman who has too much pain inside to bear sometimes."

She swallows, my thumb lingering on her lip as her eyes remain fixed on me. "I think you try to be light and funny, but maybe you have some pain too. Deep inside."

I drop my hand and stand from the bed. "We all do."

She shakes her head at me, staying in my bed. "Not like that. I don't believe anyone has a perfect life, but I've seen people who haven't experienced tragedy." Her gaze narrows, looking right through me. "That's not you."

I don't like the way the conversation is shifting and that my eyes dart to the trophies on the shelf. Her gaze follows, and then our eyes meet again. Hers hold a challenge. "They do have your name on them. I can see them now."

I shrug. "No big deal."

"Then why won't you talk about football?"

Yup, definitely don't like this. "I just don't."

"Every guy I've ever met who played football can't shut up about it, but you won't talk about it. Why?"

Christ, why the hell did I insist she talk?

"I just don't. It was a lifetime ago." I grab my phone and search, being rude as fuck, I know. But I don't stop. I look back at her. "I gotta go."

She raises one eyebrow, not moving from my bed. "Work this early?"

"No." I offer no other explanation.

This was my lesson. I need to mind my own goddamn business. Usually I do. Something about her made me want to pry, but I didn't realize it was going to go both ways. "Got a wife? A whole other life somewhere else?"

I put on my best cocky smile and grab a t-shirt from my closet, tugging it on. "Something like that." I grab a new pair of boxers from my drawer, having no shame, but just as I push yesterday's boxers down, she looks away, and I tug on the new pair before pulling on a pair of jeans. "I'm decent now."

She looks back at me but only up at my face. "I doubt that."

"Look, I know you have plans to get out of here, but I also know that takes time. Time that you're going to spend with us. So . . ." I shrug, hoping like hell she's listening to me. "Maybe you can give in a little. Share meals with us. Talk to us. Hang out."

She looks troubled. "I don't want to get too attached."

I laugh at that, unable to help myself. "We're some charming motherfuckers. I know, but still, you're already here. Maybe we can help."

I shouldn't care so damn much.

39

"You can't help me." Her voice is so fucking sad, and it tears me apart.

"Well, we want to."

She snorts, "Because you want in my pants."

My eyes narrow, taking in all her beauty, and I know she knows that's not true. "Seems to me, I could have last night. If it were only about that, I would have been."

Her eyes widen, and I watch her throat as she gulps. "You're an asshole." Her words hold no venom.

"Never said I wasn't. But Tommy and James, they really don't want in your pants, and they want to help you, get to know you. Tommy has trained several waitresses, but he never hangs out with them outside of work."

"I live here," she shoots back.

"Doesn't matter. He doesn't have to be friendly. Truth be told, he's usually not. But he likes you. James likes you. And Quinn and Logan only fuck each other, so *they* aren't trying to get into your pants."

"Finn?" she asks the question, and I smile wryly because I'm pretty damn sure if she'd have kissed him last night and tried to push him back on the bed, he'd have let her. And that thought alone pisses me off.

"Finn wants to fuck everyone."

She chuckles softly, "You?"

"I'd definitely like to fuck you." There again, her eyes widen, and she looks fucking cute when she's caught off guard by my honesty. "But regardless, I want to help you. Or at the very least, get to know you a little while we're living together."

"As soon as I can, I'm leaving." It's direct, said like a fact. And I accept that.

"I won't stop you." I grab my keys and wallet from the top of my dresser. I peek out in the hall to see it's clear before turning back to look at the beautiful, complicated goddess on my bed. "No one's out there if you want to make a break for it so they don't think we slept together."

She stands up now, walking closer to me. *God, she smells good. Citrus, I think.* Her eyes look up at me, and I see whatever she's about to say to me is hard for her. "Thank you."

"For what?"

She takes a deep breath before letting it escape. "Just thank you."

I nod my head in a reply, and she leaves my room, going straight to her own.

I wish I could say I'm going to keep my distance now, let her be strong and silent and stay away from all of us. But I know, without a doubt, that's not true.

AFTER A SHOWER and I'm changed, I go to the kitchen, walking cautiously. I can't believe I let myself fall asleep with Jase last night.

Way to go, Mya. Doing really great at that invisible thing.

I relax slightly when I see it's only Tommy in the kitchen. No one else is around. "Mornin'"

I smile and take a seat at the bar in the kitchen. "Good morning."

"Long night?" He's eyeing me closely, and I wonder if he knows. Would Jase tell him? It's not like anything happened. Not really.

Although, I swear I can still feel his lips against mine. "Not really."

"Fucking lightning is so loud up here."

Oh. Right. It stormed last night.

"Yeah, it's pretty loud," I agree as he hands me a cup of coffee.

And now, he's back to studying me because I'm acting like a scared little girl. "You okay?"

I take a drink of coffee before nodding my head and looking around the empty loft. "I'm fine. Where is everyone?"

"James and Finn are working the early shift today. And who the hell knows with Jase?" He's smiling like it's a joke, but who does know? The way he evaded my question about where he was going this morning didn't sit right with me.

I tried to joke about him having another family, but he told me nothing. *Is he hiding something? Do I care?*

"Oh," I say and drink more of the delicious coffee.

"Please tell me you don't have a crush on our Jase." His smile is amused, and I want to be mad at him. But for whatever reason, I really like him. I feel a connection to him and did almost right away.

"No. I haven't had a crush on anyone since the second grade."

He laughs at that. "Good."

"Why good?" I approach the question with nonchalance, but I'm not sure it comes off that way.

"Because you don't want to be here long, right?"

I've tried to make that pretty clear. I guess I have. "Right."

He shrugs. "Well, I don't want to see Jase get hurt."

I snort, the thought seeming so ridiculous. The man appears to be made of steel. "Him?"

He's not laughing. "Yeah. Jase is a good guy. He cares, and I don't want to see him get hurt."

"So what? You're telling me he's looking for the one?" I say it like it's the silliest thing I've ever heard.

"Maybe. I'm not sure he's actively searching."

I think about Finn and Jase that first night, the innuendos and flirtation. But then I think about how he could have had sex with me last night but didn't. "Do men like that exist?"

He laughs now and takes a bite, pushing a plate of food to me with a fork. "Yeah. They do. All I ever wanted was James. When he finally gave in and wanted to be with me, I was done. That's all I needed."

I think about what Jase said this morning about getting to know my roommates while I'm here. He told me he wouldn't try to stop me when I leave. I pick up the fork and start eating the delicious breakfast Tommy made, moaning when the omelet hits my tongue. "Jesus, that's good."

He chuckles, "*I'm* the cook."

I nod my head. "James is a smart man." I smile at him, and he agrees.

After I finish my breakfast, I head down to the bar, not stopping to chat in the tattoo parlor. Quinn is here, getting ready to open, and since I didn't see Logan in the shop, I'm assuming he has the baby. "Morning!" She sounds so chipper.

"Good morning."

"Did you sleep okay? I know the storms around here can be brutal."

I shrug my shoulders. "Nothing too crazy."

She nods absently as she wipes down a couple of tables, and I start to organize the salt and pepper shakers.

"The guys still behaving?"

I nod my head quickly but look away too fast.

Quinn prods further. "Oh God, did they do something?"

"No, not at all . . ." I smile to myself and shake my head. "I actually kind of like them."

She laughs at that and then goes behind the bar. "Yeah, they grow on ya."

"Do any of them have deep dark secrets?" The question escapes my mouth, and I wish I could reel it back in. But I want to know. I'm sure Jase is hiding something.

Her expression is cautious, her answer guarded, "Don't we all?"

That's so *not* an answer. "Does Jase?"

She takes a deep breath and turns away from me, pretending to take inventory of the bar's stock, but I know she's avoiding me. "None of them have had it easy, Mya."

"That's not exactly what I asked."

"I know, but that's all I can say. If he wants you to know his story, he'll tell you. The same way I won't divulge any information to him about you."

"Did he ask about me?" Another question I shouldn't have asked, especially because my tone made me sound almost hopeful. I kind of want to smack myself for it.

She turns back around to face me, looking suspicious. "No. I just mean I wouldn't if he did."

I nod my head. Of course he didn't ask about me. He really doesn't ask a lot of questions. "Okay. Good."

"Is something going on?"

Good job, Mya.

"No. I was just curious."

"I'm here to talk anytime you need to. I know where we come from . . ." She looks almost solemn as she looks past me, staring at the wall. "We don't always want to talk about it."

"I don't."

And I don't. Not at all.

Her eyes meet mine again. "Okay, but you can. I'm sure you're angry about what happened to Trey. *I'm* angry."

My stomach twists into knots when I hear my little brother's name. His face flashes in my memory. "It doesn't matter."

"It does." She's adamant.

"It doesn't," I say firmly, wanting to end the conversation. "He's gone. I'm gone. I don't want to think about it or talk about it because nothing can change that."

I see the sympathy in her eyes, and it threatens to strangle me with all the emotions swimming around inside of me. I just want to be numb. I want to be invisible. I don't want to be standing here with an old friend who I looked up to like a big sister talking about the death of my brother.

My brother, who trusted me.

My brother, who I failed.

Fuck, today was a long day. And it looks like it's only going to be longer when I push open the door to the loft and see it's full of people.

I recognize a lot of them. Clients who have become friends and some regulars from the bar. I look around and don't see Mya or Tommy, but James and Finn are here. *Fuckers.*

I smile when Finn walks to me, handing me a beer with the top already twisted off. "Hey, man." He points to two chicks hanging out by the coffee table that's been made into a makeshift bar. "I want the blond, but you can have the other one."

I shake my head at him, bringing the beer bottle to my lips. "I'm good."

He wraps an arm around my shoulder. "You're decent, but with a little practice, you could be good."

I shove him away with a laugh. "I told you, you aren't getting into my pants."

He chuckles at that, taking a swig from his own beer, but then his face grows slightly more serious. "You okay?"

"I'm fine," I answer instantly, not wanting to leave any doubt there.

He studies me carefully. "Okay. Now, let's party. We've earned it."

My best friend is ridiculous, but he's my best friend none the less. I go with him to at least be his wing man with the blond, even if he doesn't really need it. And I'm having a decent time for the most part, even though I'm watching the door.

Just waiting for her to get here.

She challenged me this morning, brought up some old shit I'd rather push away and not talk about, but I still can't wait to see her face.

I don't know what the hell is wrong with me.

And then there she is, walking in with Tommy, looking fucking gorgeous as ever. She's not smiling though, and for some reason, that bugs the shit out of me.

The blond chick is all over Finn, and her friend continuously drags her fingers over my bicep, signaling she wants more of my attention, but she isn't getting it. I excuse myself quickly and make my way to Mya, who's in the kitchen pouring herself some juice she bought and keeps in the fridge.

"Forgot you're not old enough to drink."

She puts the juice bottle back in the fridge and takes a sip from her glass, her eyes glued to mine. "Even if I was, I wouldn't."

"No?"

She shakes her head. "No." She starts out of the kitchen but tosses a sultry look over her shoulder. "I've found better ways to calm the noise inside."

I think I just gulped, like full-on gulped because fuck if that wasn't the sexiest thing I've ever heard, and I'm pretty damn sure she meant it to be. She heads toward her room, and I follow, my feet carrying me as if my mind doesn't have a choice.

She pushes her door open, and I'm glad no one has found their way in here yet. I follow her inside. She didn't exactly extend an invitation, but she didn't tell me to fuck off either. I close the door behind me, telling myself I just want to keep the party noise out. "And how do you calm yourself, Mya?"

Her lips pull into a sexy grin as she places her glass on the bedside table, and I sit my beer down on the dresser I'm standing next to.

"I read a lot." There's a flicker of mischievousness in her eyes because that's not at all what she was implying.

"Oh, you're fucking with me now?"

She shakes her head. She's wearing a black blouse that hangs off both shoulders, and I don't think there's any way she could be wearing a bra with that top. My mouth waters, wanting to drag my tongue over every inch of her beautiful silky skin, but I don't move.

"I'm not fucking with you. I love to read."

"I like the way you say fucking," I say as I stalk toward her. Today was shit, and I've only known this chick for a week, but I missed her today.

"And yet, you won't do the actual act of fucking."

My throat dries. I like her blunt like this. "So, you're saying you want me to fuck you?"

She bites on her bottom lip, and I fight a groan. She's so fucking sexy without even having to try. "I think I implied that last night."

I take another step closer. "I want to hear you say it."

She sits up straight, her gaze boring into me with those big brown eyes. "I want you to fuck me."

Jesus.

"We're roommates," I say, taking another step closer.

She nods. "We are, but not for long."

"You okay?" I have to ask. She looked fucking sad when she entered the loft, and we didn't leave things great this morning.

"I'm okay." She shrugs out of her shirt, revealing that she, in fact, isn't wearing a bra. And I don't think I can form words when I see her perky tits, bare and waiting for me. "I'm taking your advice and getting to know my roommates better."

"Well, fuck." I lift my shirt over my head, and I like the way her eyes roam over every inch of my bare skin. "Please tell me you have other ways to get to know the other ones."

She smirks and stands up, unbuttoning the top button on her jeans. "Yeah. I'll play board games with Finn."

My hand goes to the back of her head, my fingers tangling in her silky hair as I pull her to me, my lips meeting hers but not kissing her yet. "He's really bad at games."

She laughs and nips on my bottom lip, making me groan. "So, you aren't going to back out this time?"

"You want me to fuck you, I'm all for it. I've wanted to fuck you since you walked through the door." I pull away from her lips and look down into her eyes. "Do you want this though? Did something happen today?"

She shakes her head, but I don't miss that her eyes are glistening with tears. "I just want to forget everything for a little bit."

Fuck, I know that feeling all too well, and after today, that's all I want too. I nod as I bend to kiss her, letting my tongue drag along the seam of her lips before they part and she grants me access. She tastes like the sweet fruity drink she just drank, and I groan into her mouth, gripping her ass and pulling her legs up to wrap around me. "Condoms are in my room."

She nods her head, her arms around my neck as I open the door, peeking out and seeing the coast is clear for me to take her to my room. I lock the door and press her small body against it, my hips grinding against hers. I don't think I've ever been this desperate to be inside someone before. I'm going to come in my pants like a fucking teenager if she keeps rubbing her pussy against my cock.

I guide her feet to the ground and go to my dresser to grab a condom. I'm not going to ask her again. She's a grown woman, smart and confident. She wants to fuck me, and I definitely want to oblige.

Her hands on my jeans catch my attention as she unzips them and takes the condom from my hand. *Fuck, she's hot.*

Her lips drag down my chest as she pushes my jeans down. My cock is hard and begging to be set free, but she doesn't do that. I step out of my jeans and let her have control for now. She drops to her knees, and I stare down at the beautiful woman before me as she kisses the tip of my cock through my boxers, pulling a groan from me as I tilt my head back against the door.

"It's been a while since I've had sex."

"Nervous?"

She arches a brow and shakes her head, pushing my boxers down and eyeing my cock, making it twitch with anticipation. Her tongue darts out, licking the tip that's already glistening with my precum. "Fuck."

I feel her smiling as she opens the condom and sheathes me. I can barely take it any longer. When she stands up, my hands grip her face, and my lips crash to hers, both of us moaning with need.

I quickly push her pants and panties down as she kicks them off and we make our way to the bed. I land on the covers, pulling her body on top of mine so her breasts are pressed against my chest and my hard cock rests between her legs.

"You're so fucking gorgeous," I gasp as one hand slides over the curve of her hip and down between her legs, feeling her slick arousal. I smile, knowing she wants me too. "And fucking wet for me."

"Mmmm . . . yes," she says as I find her clit and stroke it with slow, lazy circles, making her hips buck against my cock.

She sits up, giving me full view of tits that are on the smaller side but fucking perfect and perky. Her dark nipples are hard as I use my free hand to brush over them, pulling a shudder from her small body.

My hand drags down to her belly button, and I notice it's pierced with a butterfly jewel that's sexy as fuck. "You only get hotter."

She slides her pussy against my cock, making it wet and so fucking ready to be inside her. "Fuck me, Jase."

I don't waste time asking if she's sure. I'm not a pussy, and she's not a delicate flower. But I do have a nagging worry in the back of my mind that she'll think this was a mistake after we come.

I don't worry about it now though. Instead, I position my cock at her entrance and let her slide home. And holy fuck, as she slides down my cock, taking in every hard inch, I swear I see fucking stars at the sensation of being inside her.

We both moan as she falls forward, capturing my lips. My hands grip her tits, brushing over her nipples with my thumb before pinching them with enough pain to be full of pleasure. She gasps into my mouth, and I feel her muscles clench around my dick as she moves her hips, lifting up and then slowly sliding back down. The pace is agonizingly slow, but I can take it.

I don't want this feeling to end, and if she wants to escape with me, I'm happy to help her.

She sits back up, her hips picking up the pace as my hands grip her ass, guiding her along my shaft, chasing the orgasm that's building. Her clit is rubbing my dick with each thrust, and I know she's close.

"Fuck, Mya. I'm close." One hand moves back to her clit, wanting to feel her come around my cock.

"Oh God, Jase," her moan is sultry and full of want as her hips continue to buck against me. Her palms rest on my abs as I thrust in sync with her, playing with her clit and gripping her ass, not thinking about anything but this moment with Mya.

"Just let go." And she does. She fucking does. Her body stiffens as her head tilts back and her pussy grips me tightly, not letting go as she finds her release. I topple over the edge a moment later, my cock jerking inside her as I come.

Her body collapses against mine with my dick still inside her, softening, but not yet done. I'm already craving round two.

"Holy fuck." I smooth my hand over her back and smile to myself, but my smile fades when I feel hot tears on my chest.

I slowly lift her chin so she's looking at me. "Mya?"

"I hate everything."

I stare at her, swallowing the bitter taste because I know why I feel so fucking connected to this girl and it has nothing to do with what we just did. "I know."

"You really do, don't you?"

I nod my head, letting go of her head and wrapping my arms around her body, letting her just lay on me, her head over my heart.

Maybe this was a mistake.

LAST NIGHT WAS NOT A DREAM.

I feel Jase's hard body next to mine and know that for sure now. God, his body is insane—chiseled and taut with hardened muscle, ink scrawled everywhere.

I have no idea what got into me, but when I saw him surrounded by people in the crowded loft, all I wanted was time alone with him. I don't know him. He won't tell me anything real, and I won't tell him anything either.

Yet somehow, it's like he sees me.

When Quinn brought up Trey, it just made me want an escape. An escape I refuse to get from any substance. I will not turn into my mother.

But Jase may be even more dangerous.

I turn my head and can't fight the smile when I see him dead asleep, oblivious to the world. The way he held me felt so safe. And that thought is petrifying.

I can't remember ever feeling safe.

His lips pull up into a smirk, but he doesn't open his eyes. "Ogling me?"

I roll my eyes, but after I do that, my eyes drag over his bare chest. Holy hell, he's perfect. "Nope."

"Liar." His eyes open, and he smiles at me. Jase may seem simple to some people, but to me he's a total conundrum. He appears carefree, but I see pain in his eyes. Those hazels can't hide a damn thing. And the way he understands me without any effort tells me Quinn is right. He hasn't had it easy.

"I should go."

He nods. "Right. Can't let anyone know we fucked."

He doesn't sound bitter. Instead, I think he's teasing me. "Do you really want to deal with questions?"

His shoulder shrugs. "I don't care. I give us a solid ten in the sack."

"I'm going to smother you with a pillow," I deadpan but hate how cute he is.

He laughs, "You can try. I'm pretty strong." He flexes his right bicep to prove his point, and my eyes stay fixed on the hard muscle.

"Is that where you go? To the gym?"

He sits up, pushing his fingers through his messy hair. "Sometimes."

Still vague. "I'm going to go shower. I have an early shift at the bar tonight."

"Tips suck."

I nod as I realize I left my shirt in my room. WIthout saying anything, he hands me his t-shirt, and I slip it on. "Don't get too cocky."

He yawns, "Come on, Mya. We just slept together. You know I'm cocky." He wags his eyebrows, but again, I can't argue.

"I'll see you later."

I climb off the bed, but he catches my wrist gently. "You okay about last night? For real? No bullshit?"

I nod my head. "Yeah. I needed it."

He accepts that with a nod and releases me. "Okay. Let me know if you need me again."

He expects me to say it won't happen again. I can feel it, but it was fun. Even though I had a good post orgasm cry, I had a good time. "I will."

He looks surprised as I wink at him and leave his room to go shower. My body feels deliciously sore, and I don't regret last night. Although, I feel slightly worried about him being my roommate.

And okay, maybe about getting attached.

I haven't had a boyfriend in a long time, not since I let my high school boyfriend talk me into going to the movies with him on a Friday night and left Trey with Mom. I knew it wasn't a good idea. And when I got home, she was passed out on the couch, and her fucking waste of space boyfriend was high and trying to get Trey to snort coke with him.

A sickening pain in my stomach makes my fists clench at my side. He was mine to protect, and I let him down.

I tried so damn hard to take care of him. I was so pissed-off at my boyfriend at the time, I broke up with him and ignored his every attempt of trying to get back with me. All I cared about was keeping Trey safe, and then in the end, none of it mattered.

He's still gone.

The emptiness takes over, and I climb out of the shower, getting ready on autopilot. I go to work and still feel like I'm floating in numbness.

The reprieve last night with Jase was nice, but I'm back in hell now.

"You alright?" I look over as Tommy places my drink order on my tray.

"I'm fine. Why?"

He laughs and shakes his head at me. His smile is so bright, so friendly. "You've been out of it all afternoon."

"I'm sorry." I straighten the beers on the tray, adjusting them so they'll balance. "Long night."

He chuckles as he makes a drink for another waitress. It's only six, but it's three-dollar beer night, and people are here for it. "Yeah, I saw you coming out of Jase's room this morning. I'd imagine it was."

I gape at him. Shit. I didn't see him when I poked my head out the door. "You saw that?"

He lifts an eyebrow as if to say "Why would I lie?" "Yeah."

"Shit."

He just laughs and hands off the drink to the waitress. "You're an adult, Mya. So is he. It doesn't fucking matter if you guys had sex, at least not to us."

"Us? So James knows?"

Again, he shoots me a glance, and I wave him off.

"Of course he does."

"No secrets with us. That's the rule, but it doesn't matter."

"I just don't want everyone talking about it."

"Why? Was it bad?" He fake cringes, and I roll my eyes, laughing.

"No. It wasn't bad. I just don't like the idea of everyone knowing."

A loud woman pushes her way to the bar and plops down, ordering a drink from Tommy loudly. He busies himself making it but still focuses on me. "Look, as long as you both are okay with your choices, it doesn't matter. Enjoy."

"And if I hurt him?"

His eyes darken, and I can't stop the smile from spreading on my face because he obviously cares about Jase. "Don't."

"What if I can't help it? Everything I touch turns to shit."

He shakes his head, handing the woman her drink and accepting her fifty cent tip with a smile. "Jase is strong."

"You said you're worried about him getting hurt."

"I am. I don't want to see any of my friends getting hurt, you included." He sighs, "But he's a big boy. You tell him you don't want a relationship, that you're leaving as soon as you can, and he still fucks you. Then it's just as much on him."

I nod my head, knowing that sounds logical, but in the back of my mind, I'm more afraid about myself.

And I think Tommy knows it.

"What if I get attached?" My question is a quiet whisper that makes him smile at me sadly.

"Worse things have happened."

It's not an option for me. I have to remind myself of that.

I cannot fall for him.

WHEN I GET home from work, all I can think about is Jase. Jase's body. Jase's smile. Jase's cock. His tongue.

It's annoying.

I can't stop it. I just want another taste. More moments of euphoria where I'm not thinking about loss and grief.

Tommy's right. He's a big boy, and I don't believe he's simple. He knows what he wants. He can handle a physical relationship.

I've told him I'm leaving.

He worked close to the same hours as me today, so he should be home. I walk to his room. The loft is quiet, and I peek in, seeing it's empty. I decide to wait for him on his bed, letting him know exactly what I'm here for.

Time passes, and it starts to get dark outside. *Where the hell is he? And what am I still doing here? Just waiting for a guy to come home and fuck me?*

I'm losing it.

I climb off the bed and walk to the shelf, my fingers drifting over the trophies. He really was a superstar. These aren't participation trophies. They're state and national championships.

Why doesn't he want to talk about it?

Seems to me he has a lot to be proud of.

"Mya?" Shit. Of course, now he comes home.

I turn to face him, caught red-handed snooping. "Hi."

He eyes me with suspicion but doesn't seem pissed. "What's up?"

"I um . . ." I walk toward him and away from the shelf I was just inspecting. "I . . ." Great job, Mya.

His lips lift in a cocky grin. "You're here for more, huh?"

"I don't want a relationship."

He nods his head knowingly and kicks his tennis shoes off, tugging his socks off right after. "Okay."

"I mean it. I can't . . ."

He lifts his shirt off, and I'm struck stupid staring at his ab muscles with beautiful ink covering parts of him.

"Who did your tattoos?"

He laughs, pushing his jeans down along with his underwear, leaving him in all his naked glory, completely confident and unashamed. "Why are you still dressed?"

I smile, nerves starting to get to me. I liked having sex with him. Okay . . . I fucking loved it. But the way he held me? I think I liked that even more, which is so incredibly dangerous.

That pulls a sexy, hearty laugh from him, and I cross my arms, again consider smothering him with a pillow. He stalks toward me, and I suck in a deep breath. "Don't worry, just let go."

I think about his words the first time we had sex, when he told me to let go. and I let my body relax, finding an unimaginable orgasm waiting for me. My body tingles, thinking about that. "We're both adults."

He nods his head, his finger running over the wide collar of my shirt "We are, and I'll admit, after . . ." I watch his throat move as he swallows, worry in his eyes, "the other night, I was worried that maybe I took advantage of someone dealing with crippling grief."

I stiffen, and his finger traces my bottom lip. "I'm not a victim."

His hand cups my face. "I know that. You're strong, and I sensed that from day one." His eyes are intense. "So again, why are you still dressed?"

I lean into him, my hand resting on his bare chest as I kiss him, possessing him with my mouth and letting his claim mine in return, both of us struggling for control. I'm the one who lands on the bed, pulling his body on top of mine. I just want him, and before I know it, he's inside me.

We both gasp as our mouths tangle, and he presses fully inside me. "Fuuuck." His moan is primal and sexy as hell.

"I should get a condom."

He should.

I don't want him to. "I'm on birth control, and I'd say the damage is done if you're a dirty fucker."

His hand gently tugs my hair so my eyes meet his. "I'm clean."

"Good." I lean up and capture his bottom lip with mine. "Because I'd have to kill you, and I kind of like you."

His smirk is lazy and effortless as he leans down, nipping on my neck and thrusting deeper, making my hips buck against him, taking every bit of punishment his cock has to offer.

My hands grasp his firm ass, my nails digging in as I pull him into me. Craving him. Unable to get enough. "I'm clean too."

He didn't ask, but he should know.

I feel him smile against my neck as he slams into me, my legs sprawled with him between them. I wonder how anyone could tire of this.

But I know I don't have a choice. I don't want to live in a big city.

He pulls back, looking down into my eyes. "Where are you?"

"I'm here."

He shakes his head and pulls out of me, flipping me to my stomach. I instinctively climb onto my hands and knees, moaning when he slides into me, hitting that deep delicious spot. "Oh, God."

"There you are. Stay with me."

I arch my back and bask in his touch as one hand holds my hip and the other ventures between my legs, pinching my clit. A strangled, turned-on cry escapes my mouth as he hits me deep.

"I kinda hate how well you already know my body."

"No, you don't." He pinches my clit again as I move against him at his mercy. I feel the orgasm taking hold, and my body writhes with pleasure underneath him.

There's no time for reprieve as he continues to move inside me while I come down. His hand finds my nipple and pinches, but not enough to hurt.

"Jase . . ." I push back against him as he moves forward, our bodies in sync, and it feels so damn good.

"Yes?"

My body tenses again when his cock hits the sweet spot inside and causes my eyes to pinch shut. "I'm coming again," I softly whimper as he thrusts forward, his body punishing and rewarding all the same time.

I feel his cock jerk inside as he fills me with his release. Both of us are lost in ecstasy. He pulls out of me and lays down at my side. "Holy fuck."

I smile, oddly proud as his chest fills with air and then deflates with his rapid breathing. "Yeah."

He rolls to his side, propping his head up on his hand. "I have somewhere I have to be, but I'll be back soon."

I have to ask. "Where are you going?" I give him a pointed, no bullshit look. "For real."

He stands up and grabs a pair of jeans, tugging them on. "A meeting."

I sit up, vulnerable and still naked, filled with his cum, "What kind of meeting?"

He grabs a clean shirt from his closet and tugs it on. "NA."

"Narcotics?" I feel sick. "You're a fucking addict?"

"No." He looks completely serious. He could pass a fucking lie detector test right now with how calm he answers me with his lie.

"You just said you're going to a Narcotics Anonymous meeting."

He nods. "I am. I go twice a week." He seems defensive. But if I were lying, I guess I would be too. All addicts are fucking liars.

A sinking feeling settles in my belly. "How could you not tell me that?"

He raises an eyebrow. He's fucking delusional if he didn't realize this is a big deal. "I'm sorry, I didn't know I had to go over every part of my life. You didn't fucking ask."

I fold my arms over my chest, infuriated. "I didn't realize I needed to ask if you were a goddamn junkie. I saw you drinking alcohol. Are you using again? Did you ever stop?"

He looks at his phone, making me want to throttle him. "Look, I have to go. I can't be late. I'm sorry. We'll talk later."

"No. We won't." He looks confused and maybe a little hurt, but I don't care. I'm pissed the hell off.

He studies me and starts toward me, I think to kiss me goodbye, but I move back away from him.

"Don't touch me."

"Are you fucking kidding?"

"No." I stand up, looking for my clothes and haphazardly pull them on. "This was a huge mistake."

"Mya, what the fuck?"

I hear him, but I'm already out of his room and heading toward mine.

How could he not tell me?

How could I not have known that?

I HAVE no idea what the fuck just happened. I fucked Mya bare, and then she flipped her shit. I mean, maybe I should have grabbed a condom. Maybe it freaked her out, considering we only met a week ago. But I thought we had a connection.

It unnerved me when I saw her staring at my trophies, but once I realized why she was really there, I couldn't have been happier.

I wanted her so fucking bad.

Thinking about her all fucking day. Her tight pussy was wet and ready for me. So fucking inviting, but afterward . . . Jesus. She looked like she fucking hated me.

All because I didn't tell her about attending NA meetings?

I did today. A week after meeting her. That's quicker than I've ever let anyone in. *Ever.*

"Hey, man," I say to Spencer as he approaches the old church where they hold meetings. He looks like shit, run down and way too fucking tired for seventeen.

"Hey," he grunts.

"You okay?"

"No, but I'm here."

I smile and wrap an arm around his shoulder and walk inside with him. "That's good." I'm still pissed and confused about earlier with Mya, but I'm relieved as fuck to see the kid.

I've been his sponsor for a year now, since he was sixteen and drove straight into oncoming traffic in his brand-new Mustang. Somehow he only managed to plow into a street sign and not another car, but he still did some fucking damage.

After the fancy rehab his wealthy father sent him to, he wound up in the same meeting as me. I have nothing in common with the kid—well, except reckless behavior, but I mean upbringing—and yet . . . I felt an instant connection with him.

Just like Mya.

Fuck! I need to not think about her right now. Or the way she looked sick to her stomach when I told her where I was going, how she instantly turned cold and looked like she hated me.

"Tell me what's up," I keep my voice quiet, leaning into Spence.

"Nothing. Just fucking numb."

I hate the vacant look on his face. "Nah, that's what the pills do."

"At least they felt good."

"Until they didn't," I shoot back, but he doesn't look at me. He just stares straight ahead, looking at the podium as people crowd in.

"I can't handle this shit. I fucking hate school. I hate everything."

I hate everything.

And I'm back to thinking about Mya.

"I know you think that, but you're fucking young."

"What the hell does my age have to do with it? You're twenty-five. You're young, but I know you hate life too. You put a smile on your face, but I fucking see it."

I recoil, hating the kid's words because they're accurate. I try really fucking hard to appear carefree, but I fight demons every day. I sit up straight in my chair, my long legs stretched out. "Fine. Be fucking pissy."

"I will."

Broody motherfucker.

We sit through the meeting in silence, neither of us sharing today, both stewing in our own pissed-off feelings. I'm supposed to be the mature one though, the one he can talk to about anything, the shoulder to lean on.

So, when the meeting ends and we walk outside, I don't let him off easy. "Spencer, talk to me. Did something happen? You're less pleasant than your normal sunny self."

His jaw clenches, and I nearly laugh at how angry he looks. "Fuck you."

"Yeah, yeah. Talk to me."

"It's everything. Like I said, I want to fucking use every single day, and you know what? My dad wouldn't give a flying fuck if I did, as long as I don't embarrass him."

I have no idea about the kind of pressure this kid is under. His dad is wealthy and in the public eye, a rock star of sorts. His kid landing in the news isn't great for his image even if he has a bad boy persona. It's bad PR for his teenage son to be fucked-up on drugs.

"I care."

"You shouldn't."

"I do." It's easy to say because I do.

He sighs, dragging his hand through his blond shaggy hair. "I hate him."

"I know."

"I hate this." He waves toward a car parked on the side of the street where a man with a camera is perched, not even trying to hide it.

"You hungry?"

He nods his head, and I wrap an arm around his shoulder, flipping the camera off behind my back as we walk to the car. "I can't tell you it'll get easier, kid." We climb into my car. "But you're doing well. Don't mess it up as a personal fuck-you to your dad."

"It was easier when I was high. I didn't give a fuck."

"It's no way to live." I pull out of my parking spot and head downtown to grab a burger, still thinking about Mya but glad I have the kid to distract me for a bit.

He's a good kid, and he deserves better than he got.

Never in a million years did I think I'd say that about a rich kid.

I TAKE a shower and wash Jase off me, scrubbing away the betrayal but still feeling sick to my stomach.

Am I officially my mother now?

I mean, my dad was a white tattooed junkie. From the jumbled up story I got from her, she was working and trying to save for college when she met him, fell for his shit, got hooked, and then he bailed.

Never to be seen again. I've seen one picture of my father that she keeps tucked away in a drawer, hidden from the world, trying to shield her heart from the pain he caused her.

Not that she was an innocent victim. She chose drugs and dick over everything else. She let him in.

Just like I let Jase in.

Jesus. Fuck! I let him come inside me.

I get dressed and go down to the bar, still seeing red and feeling ill. I see Quinn behind the bar and try to keep my cool, but I'm so damn hurt that she probably knew and didn't tell me. "How could you keep that from me?"

Her blond eyebrow arches as she studies me with caution. "Keep what from you?"

"That Jase is a fucking junkie."

I fold my arms over my chest, waiting for her explanation, but she just laughs at me and waves me off. "Jase isn't a junkie."

"He goes to NA meetings."

She nods her head now, and it's clear she was privy to that information. "I know."

I stare at her, dumbfounded, feeling like I'm on a completely different planet. "Quinn, we go way back. You know me. You know all about my mother. How the hell could you not tell me that?"

"That Jase goes to NA meetings twice a week? And has since I've known him?"

"Yes." I throw my hands up in frustration. "People don't go to those meetings for fun, Quinn."

She wipes the bar with a rag, her face saddened. "No. They don't."

"So how could you not tell me that?"

"Why are you so worked up?" She studies me again with guarded caution because yeah . . . I'm sure I seem a little unhinged right now. I'm out of my mind with fury.

"Because I fucked him!"

She looks at me with surprise, but no judgment. "Well, who the hell told you to do that?" She's almost laughing, and I could scream.

I plop down on the bar stool and put my head in my hands. "He's gorgeous. And fucking charming. So charming." I lift my eyes to meet hers, and she doesn't argue. "I mean . . . I just thought he was safe."

"He is safe. He's a good guy, Mya."

"He's an addict, Quinn."

She lifts a shoulder, gnawing on her bottom lip. "Maybe he is. Maybe he isn't. But he is a good man. We wouldn't be friends with him—hell, Logan wouldn't employ him—if he wasn't. But he is. He's proven himself."

I shake my head and drop my hands to the bar. "I can't believe you didn't tell me."

"Well, I didn't tell you to sleep with him. And you know, maybe some get-to-know-you questions would have been a good idea before falling into bed." She shrugs her shoulders. "But whatever. What's done is done."

"I let him inside me."

She looks sympathetic. "That's always a risk. Did he tell you anything about it?"

"No. Just that he was going to a meeting. Like it was no big deal."

She seems to think that over and then places her hand over mine. "Talk to him. Let him tell you about what happened."

"I don't want to hear it."

"You should."

"I'm leaving, Quinn." My eyes level with hers. "As soon as I can."

She nods her head, taking that in and holding her head high. "I've known you for a long time. I'd never put you in danger. Ever. Jase is not bad. I know what your mother was like. He's not that."

"Addicts are liars."

"Trust me." She implores me to listen with her gaze.

I nod my head, conceding and standing up as I take a big breath. "Okay."

She walks out from behind the bar and gives me a hug which I lean into, grateful for the comfort.

When I go back upstairs, I go straight to my room and wait. An hour later, I hear Jase's booming voice talking to Finn in the hall before walking into his room. The door closes, and I take several deep breaths. I should just let it go.

I should go on with my plan to stay invisible. Stay away from everyone. Work and save. But Quinn's eyes flash in my mind, and I think about how sincere she looked.

I wait a few more minutes and then go to his door, knocking lightly. He opens the door, a curious look on his handsome face, not flirty like he was earlier, instead almost cold.

"What?"

Okay, so that's how it's going to be. I guess I was a little aggressive earlier. "Can we talk?"

"You going to call me a fucking junkie again?"

"Are you a fucking junkie?"

His eyes narrow. "No."

I don't believe him, but I don't have the right to call him a liar. Not really. Not yet. "Can we talk?"

He moves out of the way and allows me into the room, closing the door before turning to face me. "What do you want to talk about?"

"If you're not an addict, why do you go to meetings every week?"

"To remind myself to not ever fuck up again like I did when I was younger." His eyes remain serious but then soften slightly. "And to go with the kid I sponsor who really, really needs help right now."

Don't fall for it, Mya. My heart wants to melt at the mention of him helping a young addict.

"How did you fuck up?"

He moves past me and lies on his bed, one arm tucked under his head. "Don't worry about it, Mya."

"I *am* worried about it. I'm confused." I point to my chest, pleading with him to tell me what the hell is going on. "You say you're not an addict, but you're a sponsor and you go to meetings. They don't just let anyone in."

His eyes dart to the trophies on the wall and then to me. "I'm confused. Years later and I'm still fucking confused."

I sit on the edge of the bed. "Just tell me, Jase. Please."

I don't like begging him, but I need to know because my stomach aches thinking about letting a junkie into my life. I promised myself I'd never do that.

Not that I think they aren't worthy of love or understanding, but to guard my own heart . . .

I just can't.

I LOOK at Mya as she sits on the edge of my bed, pleading with me to tell her everything. I'm worn out from the day and from life in general. I don't want to rehash this shit, but the way she's looking at me right now, it's like I can't resist.

"I had a happy childhood until I was eight." She watches me, her eyes less judgmental and cold than they were earlier today. So I continue, "My dad was a fireman, my goddamn hero. And then he died."

I see her visibly gulp, but she stays silent.

"I'll never forget my aunt picking me up from school that day. They pulled me out of class. I hadn't seen her for a while because she lived in Oklahoma. But she picked me up and told me what happened. That my dad died in a fire."

"That's awful."

I nod, trying not to let myself go fully back to that day. The memory is too painful. "My mom lost it. He was the love of her life. They were childhood sweethearts. She tried." I think about my mom, zombie-like, sitting on the couch and staring at the wall for hours. I try to shake that thought away. "Everyone said I just needed to give her time, but time didn't help her. It was like she wanted to die with him. I had to remind her to eat."

"Jesus, Jase. That's terrible." No one ever knows what to say when they hear this part, and her voice is quiet.

"Yeah. It was. She lost herself the day he died. She wasn't really my mom anymore. I was angry, but my life went on. I found football and threw myself into it." My eyes drift to all the trophies on the wall and then back to Mya. "Finn and I played football together, and he was right there through it all. I was okay."

"What happened?" She sounds almost afraid to ask.

"The town built me up like some fucking football god, and I let it get in my head. I thought I was the shit."

Now she looks over at the trophies. "I'd say you were."

I smile sadly, unable to look at them again. Instead, I focus on Mya's beautiful face. "I was good." And I was. State and national championships don't lie. "I thought maybe I could go pro. That somehow that would pull my mom out of it."

Her voice is a caress, a soft whisper from the end of my bed, "Jase, what happened?"

"My senior year of high school, the first fucking game of the season . . ." I look away from her, toward the door. "I ended up in a pile of players. On the bottom of the pile with my knee bent all the way back." She looks pained for me. "The hope was that it was just twisted, maybe torn. But the fucker was broken and bad."

She doesn't say anything still.

"I had a couple of surgeries, but it was over. The games went on without me, and I never fully recovered from it. I still fucking limp sometimes."

"I haven't noticed."

I smile at her now, but it fades. "The doctor who handled everything for me was a former player. He prescribed Oxycontin. I'd never taken anything like that before, but he said it would help. I trusted him, and I was in pain."

"You got addicted."

She says it as a statement as if all the dots are connecting now.

"I don't know."

She looks confused now, maybe a little angry. "What do you mean you don't know?"

"I mean I was pissed, so fucking pissed-off. I had no one and nothing. I had Finn, but he still got to play, go on with his life. And I resented him for it. I pushed him away, so I really had nothing." I still can't believe the fucker forgave me for that shit. "I started partying a lot, and I mean a lot. I have no idea how I got through my senior year, but I did graduate. And graduation night, I popped a couple pills and drank a shit ton."

She's watching me nervously now.

"I drove myself to a party, and I thought I could drive home."

She covers her mouth, shaking her head, preparing herself for something horrible.

"I almost made it but crashed into the stop sign by my house."

"Were you hurt?"

I shake my head. "Not really. The airbag split my cheek open, but that was it. I did get a DUI though. It was my first offense, and I was the hometown fallen football hero, so I got a slap on the wrist. Community service."

She looks slightly appalled, and she should be. I think back all the time on the what ifs. What if I'd have killed someone that night? What if they'd have been harder on my first offense? What if I hadn't wound up underneath all those big motherfuckers in that game?

None of it matters. Not really.

"Anyway. I didn't stop. I kept drinking, partying. Mixing it all with the pills they kept refilling because I told them I felt pain that I didn't."

Her hand falls to her stomach. She looks sick, instinctively knowing there's more to the story. And she's right.

"On the Fourth of July, I went to a party out at the lake, the one they had every year. I got so fucked-up, I don't remember anything except being loaded into an ambulance and seeing two other stretchers. Smashed-up cars."

Her eyes flutter closed, and I see a tear fall.

It's ripping me apart going through this again and knowing she won't ever look at me the same, but it's my reality. It happened. "I broke my arm that time and my good leg." I swallow, "and when I got to the hospital and my casts were put on, I was greeted by two officers who told me the couple in the other car should be okay, but the girl was in surgery."

She just listens to me. The silence in the room is sickening.

"Turns out, they were in the class below me. Good kids. I probably never noticed them because they were the smart kids. They weren't drinking. They went to see the fireworks. He broke his nose. She . . ." I still see their crushed car in my mind when I close my eyes and quickly reopen them. "She had a pretty bad cut on her side and broke her arm too. She needed surgery to correct it, but she was okay. They lived. I lived."

She seems to breathe a sigh of relief, but I don't feel any less guilty over that fact, that they lived. Because I could have killed them that night.

"They couldn't completely sweep it under the rug this time. So, I got ninety days in jail and two years on probation."

"You went to jail?"

I nod my head, finally sitting up to fully face her. "Yes, I did. And when I got out, I started going to meetings. I apologized to Finn, and the son of a bitch forgave me. We started taking classes to learn tattooing, and life moved on."

"So, you're an addict?"

"The counselors I've seen don't seem to think so. I don't crave it, Mya. I just don't. I can have a beer and not want anymore. I stay away from the pills. But I don't know if I'm really addicted to them or if I just fucked up during a really bad time in my life."

She shakes her head, tears remaining in her eyes. "No. You go to meetings."

"Because I never want to do that shit again. Because I'll never forget seeing those kids being loaded into an ambulance and thinking they could have died because of me."

Again, she shakes her head and stands up. "You were addicted to alcohol and pills your senior year."

"I wanted to get fucked-up, and I did. I haven't had another problem since." I stand up too, but when I approach her, she pulls back, and I stop. "Mya, why are you afraid of me?"

"Because I am." She lifts her chin. "I . . ." She takes a deep breath. "I don't think you're a bad person, but I can't . . ."

I want to walk closer but don't. "Can't what?"

"We can be roommates, maybe even friends. But I can't sleep with you anymore."

I don't get it, but I have to respect her choice. "Okay."

"My mother . . ." She shakes her head, her tearful eyes meeting mine which fucking guts me. "She's . . ." She looks about two seconds from losing it, and I know this girl is on the edge. "I just can't."

I nod my head at her, again not making a move closer to her. "Okay."

"Okay." She grabs the door handle and pauses. I think she's going to say something, but she doesn't. She twists the knob and leaves.

I lie back down on my bed and try to will away the memories dredged up by today.

I want to forget, but no part of me craves going back to any substance to do that.

I'll never do that again.

Mya

IT'S BEEN a couple days since I sat down and listened to Jase tell me his story. I still think he could be an addict, but he insists he isn't. I haven't brought it up again.

We're roommates.

And that's all we need to be.

The last thing I want is to turn into my mother. But I do think Jase is a good guy. I think it's admirable that he continues to go to meetings and he's sponsoring a young addict. I just can't be part of that world. I need to distance myself from it as much as I can.

Keep my head down and get the hell out of here.

"Hey!" Quinn places a drink in front of me on the bar with a great big grin. "So, you talked to Jase?"

She must know I did with the way she's asking. I nod. "I did."

"Good. And he told you everything?"

Again I nod. "He did. I still think he could be an addict, but I get why you didn't feel the need to warn me."

She smiles. "He's a good guy."

"Who could have killed someone from his substance abuse." I can't completely let him off the hook. I just can't.

She takes a deep breath and then sighs. "Yes, which is awful. But he's atoned for his sins. And none of us are totally innocent."

"I know."

"So how did you leave things?"

"No more sex." I'm adamant about that. She nods her head in agreement. "But we're roommates . . . Maybe friends."

"Good. So you'll be at Finn's party tomorrow?"

"Finn's party?"

She busies herself behind the bar now, grabbing more drinks as a crowd of people rush in. There was a concert tonight, and it must have just let out. "Yeah. His birthday is tomorrow. It's at the loft, and Logan and I even got a babysitter."

"You guys are all fine with Jase drinking?"

She looks like she's searching for the right words now. "Yes. I'm telling you, Mya. He's not an alcoholic. He's really not. I've known him for a long time. I've been around him at parties and here. He never, ever gets out of control."

"Until he does."

"He doesn't." She seems so certain, but there's a nagging feeling in my gut.

"Well, you know him far better than I do."

"Just go to the party. I think it will be a lot of fun."

I nod my head and pick up the drinks to deliver them. When I get back, I see Jase and Finn sitting at the bar. "There's my favorite waitress," Finn exclaims, and I shake my head at him.

"You guys don't have to work?"

"Just got off," Jase says, picking up the beer Quinn just placed in front of him, but he hesitates as he brings it to his lips. He's looking at me, waiting for me to say something. I don't. He's a grown man. If he thinks he can handle it, and all of his closest friends think he can, then that's up to him.

He finishes lifting it to his lips and takes a drink. I watch his throat as he swallows, and my eyes focus a little too long on his lips when he places the bottle back down on the bar. He eyes me, his eyebrow lifting with curiosity, and I look away.

Trying to find a table that needs help, hoping for a reprieve because this man is far too tempting.

I was doing just fine without sex. Then I had it twice with him. And now, I can't seem to stop thinking about it. About how fucking good it felt when he filled me completely. About his soft lips against mine, his strong body wrapping around mine.

Stop.

I walk toward the door to greet some newcomers, following them to their booth and taking their order, trying like hell to forget about the way Jase made me feel.

I know I seem crazy.

Maybe I am.

But I can't go there again.

Jase

"Well?"

I walk into the loft after my shift. And of fucking course, Finn has already started the party. Logan and Quinn closed down for the night just for this asshole's birthday.

I grin at him. "What?"

He punches me in the arm, a full bottle of tequila in his hand and people crammed into our apartment. "Happy birthday."

I shake my head. "It's not my birthday."

He glares at me, and I love messing with this motherfucker. "Shithead."

"Happy birthday, fucker." He hands me a beer that I gladly take and can't help myself from scanning the room for Mya. Because I can't stop thinking about her. She doesn't want me, not for sex. She says she wants friendship, but we haven't really talked since I told her about all my bullshit.

I don't get it. I'm really not an addict, although I still go to meetings to make damn sure I'm not. But she looked almost repulsed by me.

I zone in on her, standing by the large window overlooking the street, talking to Quinn. I can't take my eyes off her.

"Dude, are you going to spend the whole night staring at our hot new roommate?"

I still haven't told Finn about anything that's happened between Mya and me. Why? I'm not entirely sure. "I'm not."

"You are." He takes a swig out of the massive vodka bottle in his hand and offers me a drink.

I shake my head, but take it from him, placing it on the table. "I'm not."

"Are."

Finn may as well be my brother, but right now, I'm trying not to put the fucker in a headlock until he knocks it off. "Fine. I am." And that's exactly where my eyes are. Pinned to her in her peach dress that dips low enough to show a little cleavage but remains classy. Her hair is swept up, and she's fucking perfect, annoyingly so.

"Man, she doesn't want us. We tried."

I roll my eyes at him and take another drink. "She did." I shrug, "I mean, for like a second."

"What? You're saying she wants my dick?" He grins at me when I turn to look at him with a serious expression. He then laughs uncontrollably. "Please tell me you didn't."

"If she'd have wanted you, you would have."

"I'm different. You're the type to get all fucking attached." His hand on my chin, turning me to look away from Mya and back at him alerts me to the fact that I was already watching her again. "Point made."

"I'm not attached. I'm pissed-off and confused."

He laughs, leaning against the wall, "Oh fuck, what happened? Blow your load a little too fast? I mean, that shit happens. She's hot."

"That shit may happen to you. It didn't happen to me."

He flips me off with a laugh. "So then, what did?"

"She thinks I'm an addict."

Now he looks slightly more serious. My best friend will always have my back, no matter what. "Why does she think that?"

"Because I told her I was going to an NA meeting."

"You tell her why?"

He was there for all of it, every miserable second. I can tell he's getting defensive on my behalf. "I did. Look, man. I think her mom was, or is, an addict. She won't talk about it." I run my fingers through my hair, taking another drink of beer and watch her out of the corner of my eye, watching her trying to avoid my presence. "She thinks I'm a junkie."

"Fuck. Her." Yep, definitely defensive.

"Finn, it's a fine line."

"Nah, that's bullshit. You paid your debt and then some. You're flying right, and you haven't fucked up in years. And then she comes here and makes you question yourself." He walks over, grabbing the vodka bottle and taking another swig, eyeing Mya as he joins me again. "That's fucked-up. Her pussy had better have been amazing."

My fists clench, and my jaw tightens. "Don't talk about her pussy."

He rolls his eyes with irritation. "See? Fucking attached."

"She may not talk about her past, but we all know there was a tragedy there. Give her a break."

"And what about you?" His blue eyes meet mine, pissed the fuck off for me.

"What about me? I did that shit. You were there, Finn. I fucked up. I could have killed Mandy and Bobby. They could be dead because of me."

"They're not. They're married and fucking happy." He places the vodka back on the table and moves to stand in front of me. "You're not a junkie."

"Maybe I'm an addict."

His hands grasp both sides of my head, and he forces me to look at him. "You're not."

I look into his eyes, knowing how much pain I caused him that year, knowing how badly his mom fucked him up when she pulled all her junkie bullshit. And knowing exactly how serious he takes all of this.

"If you two are going to fuck, we can give you pointers." James is standing next to us with Tommy. They're both laughing their asses off at us.

Finn laughs, pulling me in for a quick bro hug, slapping my back and pushing me away before addressing James, "No pointers needed, motherfucker."

James laughs, wrapping an arm around him. "Please, I've heard those poor girls in your room, faking it to get it over with."

Finn flips him off and they all laugh. These assholes are my family.

I'm laughing with them when I can feel the hairs on the back of my neck standing up, feeling her. I look to where she's standing. Sure enough, her eyes are on me. Locked. But she quickly looks away.

Because in her eyes, I'm a piece of shit.

One she can't trust.

I put my beer down, tell Finn happy birthday and head to bed.

Just me and my fucking demons tonight.

Mya

HE LOOKED SO SAD when he left the living room. My whole body is on alert, and I want to go after him. *What is that?*

We haven't known each other long at all, but I hate seeing him look that broken.

I excuse myself from Quinn and Logan. I wasn't really into the conversation anyway. I was busy watching Jase.

I decide to give up and just head to my room, but Finn blocks me. I smell alcohol on his breath, but he doesn't seem all that drunk.

"Mya. Where you going?" He does, however, seem awfully pissed-off.

"To bed."

"Yours? Or Jase's?"

Oh my God. Jase told him about us? I guess I shouldn't be all that surprised. I told Quinn. I cross my arms in a defensive pose. "Mine."

"Good. Keep it that way."

What the hell is going on? Finn has been nothing but fun and flirty since I got here, but now he seems to be letting his dark side out as he glares at me. "Excuse me?"

"You heard me. You called him a fucking junkie?"

"You all think he's not an addict, but he told me what happened. Sounds like he sure lost control and was at the mercy of alcohol and pills."

"You don't know shit."

His eyes are glued to mine, offering no escape. "He told me his story. He also told me he goes to a meeting every week."

"Because he's that fucking good. There's no one like Jase. No one. He went through some serious shit. And yeah, he fucked up but owned it. How many people do you know like that? He doesn't have to go to those meetings, but he does. He doesn't have to sponsor that little dickhead, but he fucking does. He could have served his time and said fuck it, but he didn't."

Finn clearly cares a whole hell of a lot about Jase, but that could be his biggest problem. Addicts are master manipulators. And often, it's the people closest to them who are the most blind to their addiction. "I know addicts, Finn."

"So. Do. I." The way he says it, punctuating each word with intensity, and the way his eyes never waver from mine, making sure I get it sends the message clearly to me. He was close to an addict.

"Yeah? So then, you know."

"I do. I know Jase is not a fucking addict. He was a pissed-off teenager, mad at the fucking world because his dad, who was incredible, died. His mom became a zombie-like shell of herself. He thought football was his way out of that hell, and then fate came for him. He was pissed, and he used the wrong things to cope."

"Isn't that every single addict ever?"

I should have more sympathy. Maybe I do, but it's clouded by hatred for my mother. She let us down because she chose that life. We didn't have a choice, but she did. And I will always hate her for that.

"No. He's not a fucking addict. I promise you that. He goes to meetings because he feels fucking guilty for that one year of his life."

His large body crowds mine. I don't think he would hurt me, but honestly I don't know him. Still, the room is crowded. Surely no one would let him do anything to me. "Look, I didn't say I hate him and want nothing to do with him." I lower my voice, feeling slightly weird about the next thing I know I need to say, but he already knows I slept with Jase, "I just can't have sex with him."

"Right. Because he's not fucking good enough to fuck you." His hand moves forward as he grasps a piece of my hair that fell out of my ponytail. He lets it slide through his finger and thumb, snarling at me, "You can't let him between your legs again because now you know he goes to NA meetings."

I bat his hand away furiously. "I don't want him inside my body because I don't want to fall for an *addict*." I emphasize the word addict, and I watch his eyes flash with anger.

"He's not a fucking addict. I know addicts. And so does Jase." He leans in closer, his lips curled in anger and his handsome face contorted with fury. "He was there when we had to drag my mom home in the middle of the fucking night from the bar when we were twelve. Right through Main Street to my house because she could barely fucking walk and the bar was closed." I close my eyes, pained from the image. But he doesn't stop. "He was there when we came home from a grueling football practice, dirty and sweaty, and Mom was passed the fuck out on the couch, my two little sisters trying to wake her up when she had a needle hanging from her arm and all kinds of drug shit lying around everywhere. Thank God the girls knew not to touch Mommy's stuff."

"Stop," I choke out, hating the similarities between Finn's mother and my own.

"Or, how about the time I came home to some motherfucker on top of my ten-year-old sister, trying to pull her pants off?"

"Stop, Finn." I'm pleading with him, unable to take it anymore, a rogue tear escaping me. I wrap my arms around my waist and fight the sobs. "Why do people like that have kids?"

"Because they're too fucking high to remember birth control." My eyes meet his, and I see some of his anger has dissipated. "He messed up, Mya. He was in pain and didn't know how to cope. That can happen to anyone."

"So can addiction," I breathe out quietly and sadly because I don't want Jase to be an addict. I don't want to push him away, but that's all the more reason I should.

"Look, he's worked so fucking hard to right his wrongs. He's one of the good ones, Mya. Don't call him a junkie. Don't call him an addict. And don't pull him to you if you're only going to push him away. He seems light and fun, I get that, but there's a darkness under there."

"That's what I'm afraid of."

"He's not going to use again, but he will punish himself." He eases back. "He doesn't come from addicts. His father was a goddamn hero. His mother was a saint who missed her hero. It's not in his DNA, so it's not in his nature. And he wasn't raised by addicts or abused. Maybe he was a little neglected, but still, it's not nurture either. He has none of the hallmarks of addiction."

"He really just goes to those meetings out of guilt?"

"And fear." He seems to be thinking over it and nods his head. "Yeah, he's afraid he could become that. I was fucking hard on him when he started drinking and mixing it with the pills. I was a fucking dick to him, unable to handle my best friend turning into anything close to my mother."

"But you got over it?"

He nods his head, his fingers brushing over his chin. "Yeah. I did. Thank God, he forgave me for it, but that's just Jase. He fucking cares. And so help me if you crush him—"

I don't let him finish, "I won't be here long enough to crush him."

"You did the second you looked at him like he was a junkie." He leans into my ear. "Fix it."

He pushes away and leaves, heading toward a pack of wasted girls. I turn on my heels, stopping outside of my bedroom door but looking at his.

He's where I want to be, and I hate it.

Life is all about choices. I've been safe for so long and still I ended up alone without my brother.

I walk to his door and push it open, seeing him asleep on his bed. I turn and push the door closed as quietly as I can before climbing in with him, draping my arm over him.

I won't stay long. But for now, I need him.

Maybe he needs me too.

I WAKE when I feel a warm body curled against my own. At first, I think it's a drunk partygoer who's climbed into my bed. I'm not in the fucking mood for this shit. But when I turn to face her, I see Mya's hesitant smile, shining in the moonlight streaming through my window. "Mya?" I grasp her face, trying to see her eyes, but it's too dark in my room. "Are you okay?"

She nods her head slowly, still in my hold. "Finn really gave it to me."

"That sounds dirty."

She snickers at that softly, her hands moving over mine. "He was pretty pissed that I think you're an addict."

Fuck, I shouldn't have left him with that information and then retreated to my room. Leaving her alone with a pissed-off Finn wasn't a good idea. "How mean was he?"

She closes her eyes. "Not bad. He just told me the whole story, I think."

I swallow hard, thinking about the past, hating every bit of it. "His story?"

She nods, taking both of our hands with her. "Yes." She opens her eyes again. "His mom sounds a lot like mine."

I had my suspicions but despise that she grew up the same way as Finn. "His mom is a fucking waste of space. Never should have been a mother."

She nods her head sadly. "Neither should mine."

"I'm glad you and Finn are here though."

She smiles, dropping her hands to my bare chest, and I lower mine to her shoulders. "I was an asshole to you."

"You had your reasons."

She presses her lips to mine, and I experience the same fucking jolt of electricity I feel every time our lips have touched. It's a feeling I want to chase. "I can't promise anything, Jase. I'm getting out of here as soon as I can."

I nod my head, our noses brushing against each other. "I know."

The thought of her leaving kills me, and I'm pissed that Finn is right. I'm definitely all kinds of attached to this woman. "If you aren't comfortable fucking someone like me, I get it. I don't want to do anything you aren't comfortable with."

"I'm pretty damn comfortable with you."

She lifts her dress off and over her head, tossing it behind her. I suck in a breath, not used to the way she affects me. Sure, there have been plenty of women to get me hard before, but with Mya . . . It's like I don't want it to end. I don't want to break the hold she has on me. I reach behind her back and flick the hooks on her bra before she slides her arms through the straps. "You sure?"

"You'll have to let me go when I'm ready."

"I won't make that promise."

Her lips find my neck, and she nibbles. "You have to."

I shake my head, my hands falling to her hips, pulling her small body onto mine, so her silky thighs are straddling me. My cock presses against her lacy panties as it strains against my boxers. I groan, "How can I promise that?"

"Because you know my goal is to leave."

"To get out of city life."

I lazily stoke over the piercing on her belly button, and she moves her hips, sliding over my cock. "Yes. I have to."

"So, what? You want to live on a farm? A deserted old ranch? What?"

"I wouldn't go that far, but some place where the biggest case for the police is a stolen tractor or missing cows."

I laugh, pushing her panties to the side and sliding my fingers through her wet folds. Wet for me. "Sounds like my hometown."

"Don't you miss it?"

I shake my head, finding her clit and circling it slowly. She gasps and presses forward. "No."

Her hips buck forward as I stroke her. My cock is tired of talking, but I'm not. I want to draw this out as long as I can. "See," she sounds breathless, nearing an orgasm. "You're destined to be here, and I'm destined to be anywhere but."

I apply more pressure and revel in her soft whimpers. "Maybe my destiny is to be where you are."

She bites her bottom lip, rocking against me, giving me all of the control as I enter her wet pussy with one finger, sliding in and out, using my thumb to tease her clit.

"We don't even know each other, Jase."

I feel like I've known her forever. I always thought people sounded fucking stupid saying that, but now it makes sense. I don't know what I did before we met, but it feels wrong that she wasn't there. "I know you, Mya."

I thrust another finger in her, feeling her walls clench around my fingers. Her moans grow louder and louder as she rides my fingers. "You know my body."

I swirl over her clit as she clenches tightly, and I know she's coming. Her teeth gnaw on that bottom lip, and her nails dig into my chest. When she starts to come down, her body shivering from her release and goosebumps covering her skin, I push her panties off and flip us over.

I push my boxers off before pushing into her, both of us groaning as her body accommodates mine. "Jesus, Jase."

"Want me to stop?" I grin down at her with a devilish smirk.

Even in the dark, I see her rolling her eyes as her legs lift, her heels digging into my ass and pulling me even deeper inside her.

Her lips find mine. "Never stop."

I smile against her lips as I thrust into her over and over, not letting up. Something tells me we have time for slow later. I don't stop. I don't slow my pace. I'm not gentle. It's a possessive need inside of me that wants to claim Mya.

Right now, I just want to get lost inside of her.

THIS LAST MONTH, I've given in. Totally given in. I spent nearly every night with Jase no matter what our schedule is. I sneak into his room if I get off late. He sneaks into mine if he does. It's like we can't get enough of each other.

And for whatever reason, I'm just going with it.

In my old life, when I could find time to read books, I'd roll my eyes at the insta-love thing—man-sees-a-woman-across-the-room-and-must-have-her kind of bullshit—but now, here I fucking am. I can't stop thinking about him.

I've barely known him for a month, and I can't stop my thoughts from drifting to him. I crave his touch.

In the back of my mind, I know it's just a distraction. It keeps me from thinking too hard about the past, about painful, haunting memories. But when I'm lying in his arms, when we're both satiated and our breathing steadies, it feels real.

The roommates all know, and surprisingly, they don't give us that much of a hard time. It's a rare night when we're all home. Apparently, one Sunday a month, Logan and Quinn close both the shop and the bar.

It's nice. All five of us, huddled around the TV in the living room, popcorn on our laps. Well, my ass is on Jase's lap, but we share my bowl of popcorn. I hate how familiar this feels, how easy it all is.

I've never had easy in my life, and I'm just waiting for it all to be smashed to pieces. Because I know it will.

"The fucking news? Really?" Finn whines.

"It's good to keep up with current events, Finn," James, who's holding the remote, shoots back.

"Not when it's fucking depressing," Jase argues, his big arm around me, holding my body to him.

A story flashes, the red ribbon alerting us to breaking news. The headline reads "Slain Child."

No.

My body stiffens, and Jase feels it. His eyes darken as he turns to James. "Turn it."

James nods, trying to find the buttons on the remote, but I stop him. "No. It's okay." I try to slow my rapid breaths, try to stop my palms from sweating as I listen to the reporter live on the scene.

It's dark outside, but the street is lit up with red and blue flashing lights. The reporter with perfect makeup and styled hair, stands with a microphone in her hand. Her voice sounds sympathetic, but I've always wonder if that's practiced grief. Do they really care?

"The eight-year-old was sleeping when a stray bullet went through the family's home."

A tear escapes my eye when a picture of a young Black kid appears on the screen, his bright white smile shining with happiness.

"James," Jase barks out, but I'm already off his lap and heading toward my room.

I barely make it to my window before Jase's large body is behind mine.

A tear slides down my cheek, and I brush it away quickly.

"Mya . . ."

I shake my head, unable to look at him. "Don't."

"Talk to me."

My chest constricts, and I feel like I can't suck in any air. I press my hand over my heart and shake my head again. "No."

"That's it? Just no?"

I keep my voice low, hating every single memory coming to my mind, seeing blood when I close my eyes. His blood.

It's barely a croak when I turn to face Jase, determination in my bones. "Yes. Just. No."

He's pissed-off, but not enough to yell. I know his anger comes from how damn much he cares about me which will undoubtably be his downfall. This beautiful, caring man. "Mya, I want to help you."

"You can't help me."

"Not if you won't let me in."

I fold my arms over my stomach that's aching. "I've let you in."

"Your body," I quirk an eyebrow, and he huffs, "which is great, but I want more."

"I told you not to get attached to me. That's not what this is." I drop my arms and square my shoulders. "You know what this is."

"Right. Just fucking," he growls.

I nod. "And friendship."

"Friends talk to each other, Mya."

"Not about this, they don't." I don't want him to hate me. I don't want him angry with me, but I can't talk about that day. I can't talk about the past.

"I told you every fucking thing. And none of that shit was easy." I want to tell him that I didn't make him, but that's not true. I forced him to talk, he was just easier to crack. His heart is too damn good.

"I needed to make sure you weren't like my mother."

"And still, you push me away."

"This is temporary." I brace my hands on his broad shoulders and look into those hazel eyes I love. "You know that."

His arm curls around my waist, pulling me tighter to him. "I don't know that. I told you I make no promises."

"And I told you, I'm leaving as soon as I can."

The thought doesn't sound as pleasant anymore. The thought of leaving him behind actually guts me, which makes fear course through my body. I can't need anyone.

"So, talk to me while you're here. Tell me what happened to your brother."

A choked sob comes from my throat, and I push on his chest, but he doesn't let me go. "No."

"Tell me, Mya."

"You already know." I give up on pushing him away, his arms are too fucking strong, and I don't really want to get away. "He's dead."

"I know." He presses a kiss to my forehead. "But I don't know how."

"Details don't matter."

His big hand rests against my cheek, and I lean into the touch. "They do. It matters. Tell me what happened to him, Mya."

I shake my head again, leaning against his hard body, no longer fighting his touch but accepting it, praying for it. "I can't."

I hate how broken my voice sounds. My whole life, I've stood tall, tried my best to appear strong no matter what I was going through. People always perceived me as a bitch, and I preferred it that way. But with Jase . . . it's like I can't hold back.

My voice quivers, my body shakes, my eyes shed tears I've never let anyone else see.

But I don't want to be weak.

Not even for him.

SHE'S PULLING AWAY from me. I can feel it. She won't talk about what happened to her little brother. And ever since she saw that fucking news piece two nights ago, she's barely talked to me. She's used my body but been distant.

"What's wrong with you?"

I tun my head to look at Spence, who actually looks concerned. "What do you mean? I'm listening to Janice talk about giving blowjobs in exchange for crack." I keep my voice low, knowing it's rude to talk during a meeting.

He rolls his eyes at me, his eyes on the front of the crowded room, but he's still speaking to me. "You seem less cheery than normal."

I quirk one eyebrow, keeping my arms folded over my chest and eyes on the front as well. "Cheery?"

He lets out a small laugh. "Compared to me, you're cheery, always trying to get me to see the bright side of things. But today, it's like you don't have it in you."

That's because I don't. Seeing her falling apart and not being able to help her was infuriating. "We all have off days."

"Are you close to a relapse? Because I don't think I can handle that right now."

I scoff and with a huff, I drop my arms to the side. "No. I'm not. I guess I'm having girl problems."

Jesus, I want to punch myself for saying that out loud.

"Girl problems? What, are you in high school?"

Janice steps out from behind the podium and walks back to her folding chair while the guy who runs the meeting heads to the front. I lean a little closer to Spence. "No. Woman problems. What the fuck ever. She won't talk to me."

The kid looks confused now. "You want to talk?"

I almost laugh but keep it contained. "To her. Yes."

He shakes his head. "Are you fucking her?"

It feels dirty talking about Mya this way, but that's all she wants from me. A fuck here and there to keep her satisfied until she moves on. "Yeah."

"So what the fuck is the problem?"

The meeting ends, and we stand as the room starts to clear out. "I told you. She won't talk to me."

"That does not sound like a problem at all, man. That sounds like the dream. Is she ugly?"

I groan at the kid's question as we walk out of the church basement where the meeting was held. "No. Far from ugly."

"Okay, man. Then I just don't get it. You want to date? Marry her? You want her to have your bigass babies?"

None of that sounds bad at all with Mya, but I know Spencer isn't going to get that. I hardly understand it myself. "I just want to help her."

"Ah . . ." He strides toward his car, flashing his middle finger at a photographer who's pointing his camera at him while hiding behind a tree. I walk with him while he acts like he now understands. "So, you want to fix her. Now that makes sense."

"What the fuck are you talking about?"

He laughs and hits the unlock button on his car. "You like to fix things. So, this girl is broken?"

"I don't know anyone who isn't a little bit broken. Me included."

He nods his head, leaning back against his Porsche. "Exactly. You think you're full of all this wisdom and shit, but I have you figured out, Jase. The way you fix yourself is you focus on others."

"There's nothing wrong with wanting to help."

"No, there's not. But it was freaking me out, hearing you all attached and shit. Now at least, it makes a little sense."

Fucking Spence. He sounds like Finn now. "Look, asshole. I've had girlfriends before. I'm not strictly casual."

"That, I definitely don't get." He runs his fingers through his hair, and I laugh.

"You're young."

"So are you. Far too young to be hooked on one pussy."

"Let's talk about you." I lean against his fancy car, standing next to him.

Now he groans, "No."

I laugh, "Still having daddy issues?"

"He wants me to move away, somewhere less populated. I think if he could convince a nice Amish family to take me in, he fucking would. Anything to keep me out of his hair."

An image of this spoiled kid—who's used to getting the newest iPhone before it's available to regular people and eating with a silver spoon every night—dressed in all black with no technology comes to mind, and it is not pretty. Still, I laugh, "now that would be fun."

"He'd fucking do it."

"You'll be an adult soon, kid."

"It doesn't matter. If I want him to pay for college, I have to do what he wants."

"Stay sober."

"Be perfect."

I feel his sadness and hate how miserable this kid is. "You want to come over for dinner Friday?"

"With Finn?"

I laugh, almost forgetting the two don't get along. Like Mya, Finn doesn't have much tolerance for addicts, but the fact that Spencer is a spoiled rich kid makes it even worse. "I'll tell him to behave."

He shakes his head. "Nah, I'd rather get my dick wet. A nice girl from school invited me to a party."

I doubt she's that nice. Spence doesn't do nice. "Make sure you wrap that dick."

"Yes, Dad," he mocks as we move away from his door, and he pulls it open. He climbs in but doesn't shut the door yet. "Just give her time. Talking isn't everyone's strong suit, but you're really fucking good at wearing people down."

I smile and shut the door for him, giving him a nod and wave. He speeds out of the parking spot, and I walk to my own car.

Mya needs space. It's against everything in me, but I know I need to let her come to me with this one.

I HATE the distance I feel with Jase now. I know it's my fault. But I still despise it. After his body pulls away from mine, both of us coming down from release, the distance is even more apparent.

He lies on his back next to me, looking up at the ceiling.

"Jase," my voice is quiet. Scared.

"Yeah?"

"Why are you so nice to me?"

He laughs softly, rolling to his side, and I see his bright smile in the dark room. "Why does everyone think I'm cheery and nice?"

I roll to my side to face him. "I never said cheery."

"Spencer thinks I am."

I smile and let my fingers drift over the stubble on his chin. "You're just . . ." I feel sobs bubbling up in my throat, and I try to push them down. "You're so good."

"I'm not good, Mya. I've done some bad shit."

"But you care. You care so damn much. I'm . . ." His hand rests over mine, so large and comforting. He makes me feel so damn safe. "I'm cold, and I try to keep people away. Why can't you just use my body and let me go?"

"I see you, Mya. The real you. And you aren't fucking cold. And I'm not fucking nice. I just really . . ." his hand moves from my hand to my mouth, his thumb tracing my bottom lip, "really like you."

I smile, a tear sliding down my cheek. "I don't want you to like me."

"Yeah, I got that." His smile only adds to my comfort. "But I do."

"I'm hard to love."

He laughs at that. The bastard actually laughs. "You're not hard to love in the slightest, Mya. You've just been surrounded by assholes your whole life."

I choke on a cry, fighting it. I don't want to cry. I want to stay wrapped in his happiness and warmth. "Everyone leaves."

His hand drops to my waist, pulling me into him. "What do you mean?"

"My dad left before I was born. Quinn, Rhys, Sean, and Logan. They all left. My mom was never there, even when she was." A warm tear slides down my cheek, but I keep going. "Charity," her name is a sad whisper as I close my eyes and picture her once bright smile. "She was my best friend in the world, and she left without saying a word to me." He holds me closer as I start to sob. "And then Trey left."

I don't want to think about this. The pain is too great.

But I force myself to go on when he doesn't ask. He doesn't try to force me to talk. He just holds me.

"He trusted me. He knew from a young age, like I did, that we couldn't trust Mom. When we'd go to the grocery store, on the rare occasion Mom actually bought food, if the cashier asked if he could have candy, he'd look to me for approval. Not her. Never her. He was always looking to me."

His hand slides gently over the bare skin on my hip, calming me, but I continue to cry. "You were a good sister."

I shake my head. "Until I wasn't. He trusted me so damn much, Jase."

I feel his hand under my chin as he tips my head to look up at him. "What happened?"

"I had a job as a waitress in the shitty little diner near our apartment." My chin wobbles with the sobs that are about to take over my entire body. "I was so tired when I got home that evening. Trey had been cooped up inside and had so much energy." He was smiling so big when I came home. My heart aches in my chest, but I keep going. "So much damn energy. We didn't have a lot for him to do, and he begged me to let him go outside and play."

His hand smooths over my hair, and my tears fall.

"I shouldn't have let him, but I was so damn tired."

He holds me closer, and I want so badly to get lost in him. But I'm back at the shitty apartment—a one bedroom for three people, brown water coming out of the leaky faucet, the smell of mold and rot.

"I told him he could go outside for twenty minutes while I stayed on the couch with a book." I let out a strangled cry, thinking about the next moment that I play over and over in my head. "I must have fallen asleep. But I was woken up by a loud sound, a bang and then another."

"Fuck." His voice is a harsh whisper.

"I ran outside, but I was too late. Trey was lying there, lifeless, blood seeping from his chest. He was already gone, but I still pulled his body onto my lap and rocked him, begged him to come back, told him how fucking sorry I was. I knew it wasn't safe for him to be outside in our neighborhood. But I let him."

"He was a kid, Mya. That wasn't your fault. He should have been able to play outside."

"But that wasn't our reality, Jase. And I knew that. I just wanted a few minutes to myself to read and rest. Look what it got me."

His arms wrap around me as he pulls me flush against him, letting me sob against his chest. Warm. He's so warm. And safe.

"It wasn't your fault, Mya."

I cry harder when he says that, and he only holds onto me. Taking my pain. Wrapping me in warmth and kindness when all I can offer him is my bitter coldness.

"What happened afterward?"

I try to force away the memories. The ambulance and the cops pulling up. Them taking him out of my arms. Trying to get me to calm down as I wailed into the night. "They took him away. And then the media came. Fucking flies to the corpses. It was the sixty-second murder that year in the city."

I rest my hand on his bare chest and feel his heart.

"That's awful."

I nod. "The press wanted their story. It was a big one. The community rallying together to prevent violence. Pastors on the screen telling people it needs to stop. Grieving mothers used for ratings, sobbing and telling their stories." I look up at him, knowing I sound distant and bitter because I am. "They didn't care. It all fades. Soon there's another crime. Another victim. Lottery winner. Sports team victory. They all move on, and I'm still without my brother."

He's careful with his words. "I'm sure they wanted the story and the ratings, but I have to believe they also want change." I'm about to argue when his hand caresses my cheek and holds it. "Or someone watching wants change. Wants better for the world. Maybe your little brother's story will spark that change and will hit the right person and will make a difference."

"Nothing ever changes."

He shakes his head. "That's not true."

I want to believe his words, believe that someday there will be less crime, that human beings will treat each other with decency. But everything I've seen up until now makes that thought seem hopeless.

"It is, Jase. I want out of the city. I want to feel safe." Like I do in his arms.

I try to push that thought away, though, because this is temporary. This will fade. He'll grow tired of my attitude.

"There's good and bad everywhere. It doesn't matter where you live, Mya. But if you want to live in a small town after the hell you've been through, living in the city, I get that."

I let more tears fall before wiping them away. "I miss him." My voice shatters talking about Trey. "I miss him so much."

He hugs me to him again, resting his chin on my head. "I know."
There's nothing left to say, nothing I haven't told him.
I resent the safety his arms provide.
Temporary.
It's only temporary.

JESUS, I knew it was bad, but not that bad. Who the fuck shoots a kid? I feel her agony but have no idea how to help her, so I just hold her.

If I could take away her pain, I would in a heartbeat.

"Do they know who did it?"

Her head shakes, and it's still buried in my chest. "No," she scoffs, jaded and tired. "They're never going to find out. People around where I grew up, they don't talk to the police. They don't rat."

"Even if it's about an innocent kid's murder?"

I feel her tense and think maybe I should just shut up, but her head tips to look up at me. "It doesn't matter who the victim is, there's always someone protecting the wicked."

I have to believe justice will be served. My dad was a fireman in a small town. He was friends with a lot of cops, a lot of good men. Men who checked in on me and my mom after he died. I have to believe they'd want to solve a murder, but I'm not naïve. I've seen the news and have been in Nashville for years. Murders go unsolved all the time. Corrupt shit happens.

"I'm sorry, Mya." There's nothing else to say about it, no way to make her feel better. He's gone, and she blames herself.

"You go to meetings because you feel guilty about the wreck?"

It's a question but said like a statement because she already knows the answer. "Yeah. I think about it all the time. How I could have ruined people's lives."

My stomach clenches, thinking about my first thought after the wreck. What my father would think. First responders who knew him were at the scene. He gave his life to save others, and I could have taken innocent lives.

"Sometimes I think that maybe the guy who killed Trey feels guilty about it."

I kiss the top of her head as I think about her statement. "How could he not?"

Her eyes meet mine. "Not everyone is as good as you, Jase. Some people are just bad."

"It had to be an accident, right? I mean, there's no way your brother was an actual target. Maybe they were aiming for someone else or being stupid and reckless. Who knows? But maybe there's enough guilt they'll turn themselves in."

"I can't let myself hope for that. I've seen it too many times. No one comes forward."

We stay quiet. Her head rests against me yet again, and I try to change the subject. "Tell me about Charity."

I feel her smiling against me before she lifts her head to look at me. "She was my best friend since we were tiny. Both born on the shitty side of town to people who should have never had kids." Her smile brightens. "Still, she managed to be so carefree, and she had this insanely infectious smile."

It's so damn good to see Mya have fond memories when it seemed like they were all dark.

"She always found a way to be happy, no matter what. I was always the serious one."

"She just left?"

Her smile fades now. "Yeah. She'd been in a horrible home. She wouldn't talk about it or tell me what happened to her there. She became distant, and then she just disappeared on her eighteenth birthday. Not even a good-bye."

Jesus, her fucking story is heartbreaking. "Nothing since?"

"No. I tried to file a missing persons report, but they said she was a runaway."

I try to tread lightly. I don't know Charity, and I'm sure it's a sore subject. "Do you think she did? If she was living in a bad place, I mean?"

Her shoulder lifts. "I don't know. Maybe."

"I won't leave." Her eyes meet mine, and I see her swallow when she sees I'm serious. "I'm not going anywhere."

"But I am."

I still can't wrap my mind around that. I think I'm hoping she'll change her mind, but even after only knowing Mya for a little while, I know that's unlikely.

"I couldn't help Charity. I couldn't help Trey. I just want to escape, never get close to anyone again and fail them again."

"I can't imagine you failing at anything. The world seems to have failed you, and the system did as well, but not you. You're as close to perfect as I can imagine."

Her lips brush over mine, and I feel her smile against my lips. "I'm not perfect."

"To me, you are."

I didn't expect anything like this. I've dated a few women. I've had one-night-stands. But nothing in this world has ever compared to her.

It's been a couple of months since I gave in and finally told Jase the whole story about Trey. Since then, I've told Quinn and Logan too. They, of course, didn't know what to say, but it was always a cold reality in the neighborhood where we lived.

I don't think they were shocked to their core like Jase was. Still, he doesn't seem to look at me any differently.

I've tried my best to get some distance from his heart and mine, but it feels nearly impossible now. His touch is my addiction. His laugh and smile are my cravings. And I get a hit any time I can.

"So, why don't you sing anymore?"

I gape wide-eyed at Quinn, who's just kicked everyone out of the bar and locked up. It's just Jase, Tommy, her, and me inside the bar as the guys situate the tables and chairs back into their places.

"I just don't enjoy it like I once did."

She nods her head sadly, and I sense Tommy and Jase are listening. "I'm sorry. I know what that's like, but don't forget how much you once loved it."

I loved Quinn's music lessons when I was a kid. Loved. Them.

It was one of the rare times I would feel like smiling when she'd play her guitar and teach me the notes. New songs.

But then I grew up. Had to get jobs to help keep the lights on, take care of Trey. And singing became a useless hobby that went on the backburner.

"It was just something to do."

Her eyes slide to the small stage at the back of the bar. "Wanna do it now?"

My whole body feels tense at her offer, and I shake my head quickly before moving to wipe down the sticky tables.

Of course, Jase heard and is by my side in a second. "Wait? You're gorgeous, funny, just enough of a ballbuster to keep me on my toes, *and* you can sing?"

I roll my eyes at his over-the-top ridiculousness. "No. It was just something I did with Quinn when I didn't want to go home." I shrug my small shoulders, dwarfed by his large presence and feeling uncomfortable by the subject. "Trey liked to hear me sing."

His face turns less enthusiastic now, and his voice gets quieter, "I bet he'd still like to hear it."

"Your voice was effortless, Mya," Quinn is hesitant to add.

None of them really push people into doing something they don't want to do, but hell if they aren't the most charming people on the planet.

I look back at the stage with the single microphone standing in the middle. I love the simplicity of that stage. I toss the rag on the table and look over at Quinn.

"One song can't hurt, but I'm extremely rusty."

She grins at me, already jumping on the stage. Quinn sells out venues all over the country, but she seems incredibly eager to hop on that tiny stage in her bar. Jase gives my arm a simple squeeze, but the gesture is all I need.

I walk up on the stage with Quinn as she grabs her acoustic guitar and strums the chords gently, a huge smile forming on her face, one I feel all the way down to my toes. Music has healing properties that nothing else in this world holds.

She starts playing a song familiar to me, one she taught me so long ago that I would sing over and over on my walk home, in the shower, and in the halls at school. I wanted to perfect it.

As the opening notes to "Landslide" by Fleetwood Mac sound, I feel a warm feeling drift through my body that I haven't felt in a long time.

A tear threatens to escape as Quinn nods toward the microphone. Tommy and Jase sit down in the chairs right in front of the stage. My heart is thundering, but I take a deep breath and the lyrics come to me in an instant.

I think about Trey and the way he would calm down when I'd sing to him. I think about all the fucked-up times our mom would get high and abusive or worse, or when one of her boyfriends would, and we'd lock ourselves in the small bathroom in the apartment and I'd sing to him, soothe him the only way I knew how.

And he'd calm down, lean against me. I wanted to do that the day he died, sing to him and make it better. But nothing could make it better.

I choke out the first note. And then another. And before I know it, my eyes are closed, and the room is filled with the sound of Quinn's guitar and my voice. She doesn't sing with me. She just provides the background music as I sing my heart out.

Thinking about Charity and how happy she was when we were growing up, how I used to give her a hard time for being so damn bubbly. And then the first time I saw a bruise on her arm, then on her neck. How pale and malnourished she looked. I saw the light slowly seep out of her. And then she was just gone.

I think about my mother and walking in on her, dead to the world with needles hanging from her arms, her clothes dirty, and her body weak and worn, letting drugs and horrible men into her body. How numb she always looked. I think about how maybe she had that same light once but let it all go.

And I just pour every single feeling into every note I sing. I push my vocal chords to expel the hate I have for her, for the person that took my brother away, for whoever hurt Charity. The bitterness I feel toward her for not talking to me. I let the music cleanse my soul with every single beautiful word.

And when Quinn stops playing and my final note ends, I open

my eyes to lock onto Jase's hazel one. He's watching me like I'm the most beautiful thing he's ever seen. And when he smiles, I feel it deep inside.

I have no idea how I'm going to get out of his hold.

Jase

HER VOICE.

Holy shit.

I've never heard anything like it. Sweet and soulful, but full of sultry gravel. Fucking perfect.

When she said she used to sing to her little brother, I could understand why the subject of her singing hadn't been brought up, but I can't imagine never hearing that sound again.

"I told you. You're fucking perfect," I growl as I drag my lips down Mya's throat. Her small body is currently pressed against the wall in my bedroom.

"You're insane."

I chuckle as I find her lacy panties under the skirt of her dress and slide them down her toned legs, kneeling before her. Her hands find my shoulders, her nails digging into the skin as my mouth finds the inside of her thigh.

"Your voice does crazy things to me."

I feel her laugh, but it quickly turns into a gasp when my tongue finds her slit. "Already wet for me." I find her clit and circle around it. "I fucking love that."

She moans softly, her fingers sliding through my hair, pulling me into her. "Yes."

I press one finger into her, marveling at the way she grips me

115

and then I slide another in. Her hips buck forward, chasing release. I want nothing more than to give it to her.

I watched her on that stage. I listened to every single note she sang. Maybe she doesn't love singing like she used to. I'm certain she isn't looking to be famous, but I heard every bit of emotion she expelled through each note.

Every lyric she sang held her anguish. It was like watching someone break free, even if it was only for a moment.

And it was a beautiful thing.

It's nearly the same as when she comes. She allows something—someone—to take her pain away. I'll be that for her for as long as she lets me.

Her hands curl into my hair as I lick her, bringing her body closer and closer to pleasure.

I laugh against her, causing her to moan. I let my hands slide to her firm ass, pressing my tongue into her. Her hips again buck against me, fucking my tongue, and I groan, my cock aching to be inside her, jealous of my own fucking tongue.

"I should be bored with you by now," she moans softly, her nails digging into my scalp.

I don't want to hear that and decide to punish her clit. Moving my mouth to the bundle of nerves, I suck it into my mouth, causing her to shudder.

"Fuuuuck. Jase."

I move back to a gentler touch, circling with my tongue and then switch back to sucking before nipping gently with my teeth. She lets out a surprised squeak, and I swiftly soothe the ache with small circles.

"I'm going to come," she moans, her fingernails now in my neck.

I don't let up now, licking her clit as she bucks against me, writhing. Her moans harden my dick until I can't fucking take it any longer. She's barely over the orgasm before I stand, lifting her dress off her, mashing my lips against hers.

Her hands find the button on my jeans, and she has me naked before we make it to the bed. Her legs part for me, and I thrust inside, unable to get enough of Mya. Her constant reminder that this is temporary only adds to the frantic feeling I have as I slide inside her over and over.

Her pussy clenches around me, and her heels dig into my ass as she pushes me deeper inside, and I know she's fighting the same battle I am. I fucking need this woman like I've never needed anything else. I take her as she gives herself to me.

She says this is temporary. I know she believes it, but I'm not letting this girl go.

We both lie on my bed on our backs, panting, sweating, and sated.

Even at the worst part of my life, I didn't feel as out of control as I do when I think about her leaving. *Would I even survive it?*

"Please tell me you plan to sing more often?"

Her body is suddenly wracked with laughter as I turn to look at the most beautiful fucking sight I've ever seen. Mya, completely naked, freshly fucked, and laughing freely. "Well, if you'll fuck me like that every time I do, I suppose I should."

I laugh slightly but become serious and roll to my side. "You stopped after Trey died?"

Her smile fades, looking up at the ceiling. "I sang to him, but I stopped taking lessons with Quinn long before that. And singing in the shower, singing for me."

"So, you only sang for him?"

She nods her head.

"You sing like you love it." I tuck a piece of hair behind her ear, and she presses my hand to her cheek.

"I do, but I also hate it." She turns her head to look at me, her cheek resting against my hand. "It reminds me too much of my mother's voice. She had a beautiful voice."

I know she hates her mother. "Seems like she gave you at least one gift then. Don't hide it."

She shakes her head. "She wanted to be famous, so badly. She craved fame and went to clubs, begging for someone to pay attention to her. That's how she met my junkie father and became one herself. She never became famous, but she found a new love."

"That would never happen to you."

She sighs softly, her chestnut eyes digging into my soul. "I never wanted fame. Never. I love being on a small stage, singing my heart out. But I've never craved being on the big stage."

"So, you'd be happy singing only for me on a small stage forever?" I grin, and she brushes her hand over the stubble of my cheek.

"I think I would."

And there it is.

Not temporary. She wants me too. I lean in, pressing my lips to hers. "Good, because I can't imagine never hearing that sound again."

I feel her swallow tightly, her lips pressing a kiss to mine, her breath so soft. "Yeah, I'm pretty sure I could sing to you forever."

I kiss her, my body against hers, holding her to me.

I'm not letting her go.

Mya

"YOU AND JASE TOGETHER?"

I look up from my cereal, barely awake, and stare at Finn. "What?"

"You heard me." He leans over the counter, still shirtless from sleeping. His hair is messy, and I see claw marks on his shoulders.

"Is your little friend still in your room, Finn? Does she think you're bringing her breakfast in bed?"

He offers a wicked grin, looking over his shoulder at the marks. "Fucking catlike claws." He shakes his head. "And no, I left her place and came back here to sleep."

"How romantic. So, she'll wake up alone after fucking you, and you want to interrogate me?"

"I'm not fucking your best friend." His eyes narrow. "So, how about you answer me."

I kind of hate Finn. I know he's Jase's best friend. I know Tommy and James love him, and so do Quinn and Logan. But I really kind of fucking hate him.

And then again, I don't. I know he went through similar things that I did.

"We sleep together every night."

"I'm not asking if you let him between your legs. I know that. I'm asking if you're together. If you're in love with him."

My heart squeezes tightly in my chest as I place my spoon in my cereal bowl. *Love.* Love has only ever brought me pain.

I don't want to love anyone.

I loved my mother. She broke me. I loved Charity. She fucking left me. I loved Trey. He died.

A tear falls from my eye, and I despise that moisture sliding down my cheek, making me seem vulnerable.

"You are, aren't you?"

I hate this bastard.

I don't say anything. I just fold my arms over my chest and sit up straight, locking eyes with him.

A sly smile forms on his lips. "Good. I'm glad."

"You're glad I love him? I thought you wanted me to stay away from him."

"No." He shakes his head. "I said don't hurt him. I don't want to see him hurt. You love him though."

"I can still hurt him."

His gaze darkens. "Don't."

I drop my hands and stare at him. "I don't want to."

"Then don't. Just don't fucking run. He knows you don't want to be here. I'm pretty sure he loves you too."

"We barely know each other."

He rolls his eyes. "Please. He knew you the moment he saw you. He's good at that."

I smile. "You're kind of in love with him too, aren't you?"

At this, he chuckles and grabs juice from the fridge, turning back to face me. "I treated him like shit when he needed me the most. He was struggling, and I pushed him away."

"You had your reasons."

I watch him swallow, his Adam's apple bobbing in his throat uncomfortably. "It wasn't right. He'd always been there for me. Always. And when he needed me, when I could have returned the favor, I left him behind. I was a scared little bitch who couldn't handle seeing him that way."

I'm not sure I could have either.

I close my eyes, fighting more tears and take a deep breath. "I lost my best friend too. She left, but she never came back."

I open my eyes and find his intent on me. "She died?"

I shake my head slowly. "I don't know. She just left. I knew she was in trouble, but I didn't make her talk to me. And she left." Pain spreads throughout my heart, and it's unbearable to think about Charity. "I won't just run away from Jase. I know that pain."

He nods, grabbing a glass and pouring juice. "I don't trust many people, but I believe you. Don't make me into a chump."

"Too late." We both turn as Jase walks into the kitchen. He's grinning at Finn. "You've been a chump since I've known you. What are you guys talking about?"

Finn plays it cool, returning the juice back to the fridge. "Wouldn't you love to know?"

He wags his eyebrows, and I roll my eyes. But then I see Jase is holding my phone. He places it next to me. "You have a missed call."

I look at the number and huff, locking my phone and taking a bite of my cereal.

I see the men share a look before Jase takes a seat next to me. "Not important?"

"It's a Kansas City number. I'm sure it's just a reporter. They probably had another shooting and want to rehash all the old ones, really pull at the heartstrings."

Finn takes a gulp of the orange juice and wipes his mouth. "Isn't that good? More press. Maybe they'll find out who killed your brother."

I feel Jase's body tense next to me. "Shut up, man."

Finn has no filter. Something else to hate, but I actually like that more than the constant coddling. "It's okay. I can talk about it. But no. Because they don't care. It just adds more weight to their story."

"Well maybe it'll lead to more info." Finn leans his elbows on the counter, facing me and Jase.

"No one is going to talk. No one who actually knows. It's code."

"A code that protects child murderers?" He raises an eyebrow, and I notice Jase's hands forming tight fists.

"That's fucked up."

I don't argue, but I don't want to think about this either. "It is what it is."

Finn finishes his juice and puts the glass in the sink, looking at Jase, "I have the early shift. What about you?"

"Nope. Late shift."

They bump fists, Finn gives me a tight nod and then leaves. I slowly take bites of my cereal and feel Jase's gaze on me.

"I'm sorry. I'm sure that's a shitty thing to think about first thing in the morning."

"Not the best." I take a bite and turn to him, crunching my cereal. "It's okay."

"You working the late shift or the early one?"

I smile. "Late."

His hands find my hips as he leans in, dragging his mouth over my neck. "Good. Seems like you're mine this morning then."

I sigh, leaning into him. One hand slides under my thin tee and over the lacy cup of my bra, and my lips seek his. My eyes close just as his lips meet mine.

"You know, I could eat breakfast without seeing Mya's tits."

Jase groans against my mouth, and I laugh when I hear Tommy. My hand presses against Jase's chest slightly, urging him back. "Good morning to you too."

He smiles. "I'm sure they're lovely." I laugh again as he walks to the stove, eyeing my bowl of cereal. "You guys want a real breakfast?"

Jase slowly slides his hand out of my shirt. "They're fucking fantastic, and yes."

Tommy laughs, winking at me as he grabs a frying pan. "You guys hear the forecast? Severe weather."

"Fuck," Jase grumbles as I finish my cereal that Tommy clearly disapproves of.

"Is it always storming here?"

Jase and Tommy give me a simultaneous, "Yes."

Jase's strong arm wraps around my waist. "So what are we going to do today?"

Tommy seems intrigued. "You guys have the late shifts?" We both nod as he cracks some eggs. "Fuckers. I'm already late to work."

I laugh because he's still here making breakfast. I suppose this is Logan and Quinn's fault for hiring friends.

I turn to Jase. "I wouldn't mind being shown around town."

He looks surprised by that. I haven't wanted to go out since I moved here, always saying how much I hate the big city. It's still true. I still want to live in a small, safe town, but one thing has changed.

Jase.

I don't want to leave him.

"Jesus, is that hail?" Mya asks, and I nod just as I'm pelted in the face with icy rain.

"Yup, come on." We just got back from exploring Nashville and are climbing out of my car. It seems we're just in time because the pouring rain has turned into hail.

When she said she wanted me to show her around today, I thought for sure she was fucking with me. She hates it here. She wants out, but I took it and ran.

We went to the Musicians Hall of Fame because I was pretty sure she didn't want to go to the Grand Ole Opry. And lord knows, I didn't want to either. But the Hall of Fame was badass. Then I took her downtown and out to a nice dinner.

It was in the back of my mind that if maybe, just maybe, I could make the city bearable to her, she might stay.

God, I want her to stay.

Of course, the fucking weather isn't working with me.

The sky lights up, and then there's a loud crack of thunder. "Fuck, that's close." I usher her inside, and we head up to our place. I flick on the lights, and Mya moves to the large window, looking out.

I move behind her. "Don't you know you're supposed to stay away from windows during a storm?"

She sighs and leans back into my body. "I've never been able to avoid the storm before."

I know she's speaking metaphorically now. "Still thinking about that KC call?"

She nods her head, still staring out the window. "I was never afraid of storms. Never. We had them. Some were pretty damn severe, but I wasn't afraid. We had to stay away from the windows to avoid bullets. Could never go outside when it was dark. Could never walk alone at night. So many rules where I grew up."

It's amazing the things she's endured. My mother warned me about glass breaking during a storm. Mya was afraid someone would shoot her in the place she should have felt the safest. "No wonder you hate the city."

"This is pretty nice, though." She turns around, wrapping her arms around my neck. "I wasn't afraid today."

I smile, letting pride surge through me. "I'll never let anything hurt you."

"Some things are impossible to stop."

There's another flash of lightning and a loud crack, killing the lights and leaving us in darkness. She flinches from the loud sound.

"Fuck, power's out."

She nods against me, and I think she's about to kiss me, but then the hail picks up, hitting the window with a fierce attack. Then I hear the sirens.

Fuck.

"Tornado."

"What?" Now, she sounds frightened.

I take her hand. "Come on. It's okay. There's a basement in the bar."

I wonder if everyone's already there. I haven't checked my phone, having ignored it most of the day. If there was a weather alert, I had no idea. Mya uses hers to light the way as we walk down to the bar and find it empty. I find the door to the basement and tug it open, seeing Tommy, Logan, and James when we walk down the stairs. It's lit up with a lantern and a few candles.

"Where the fuck is Quinn?" I look to Logan, who's gritting his teeth.

"At home with the baby." He's fucking worried.

"She'll be okay. She in the basement?" He nods. "Where's Finn?"

He shrugs. "Fucker won't answer his phone."

God damn it.

I turn to Tommy, who grins. "He went home with some skanky looking chick. I'm sure she has a basement."

"She better." I take a seat on the bench they moved in here for just this occasion.

Mya takes a seat next to me. "Do you think it's bad?"

James hands her a bottle of water. "They said it has potential to be. Where the hell have you two been? We called."

We share a look, and I shrug. "Tour of the city."

"Is that code?" Tommy wags his eyebrows.

I laugh. "I wish."

Mya playfully punches me, but really my mind is on Finn. *Where the hell is he? That fucker better be okay.*

"Shit." I turn to Tommy, who's looking at his phone. "It's bad." He holds up a grainy Facebook Live video from a local station of a tornado having touched down.

"Fuck." I watch as it rips through main street. "That's right here."

He nods grimly as we hear the sounds from the storm above us inflicting damage.

Mya looks up at the stairs as we all huddle together, and I hope it passes soon.

Moments later, the tornado is gone, but it's torn everything apart. We were trapped in the basement, the debris blocking us in. How we survived, I'm not sure, but thankfully we were able to reach help. It takes Fire and Rescue to open the door to the basement, releasing us from what could have easily been our graves.

As we come out of the rubble, I peer through what used to be the bar. It's wrecked. The windows are shattered. Tables are everywhere.

The brick has fallen in shambles. It's amazing how something so brief can do that much damage.

We all stare, stunned, as Logan calls Quinn frantically.

He reaches her and tries to find a quiet spot to talk to her in the chaos. There are news crews and people everywhere, assessing the damage. Mya looks up at me, tears in her eyes. "It's gone."

I nod, looking over at the tattoo shop that's in even worse condition than the bar. "Yeah."

She shakes her head slowly. "I was just starting to like it here."

I laugh at that, tugging her to me, wrapping my arms around her. "It'll be okay." I'm sure she didn't like admitting that.

I grab my cellphone and call Finn but still get no answer.

Please let him be okay.

"He didn't answer?" I shake my head, and she leans against me. "He will."

"I hope so." There's a sick feeling in my gut.

"He will. He's strong. And kind of a pain in the ass. I'm sure a tornado can't take him down."

I smirk, but then my mood quickly sours, looking around at the wreckage around us. The entire street is leveled. Businesses that have been here for a century are just gone. People's life savings, blood, sweat, and tears have been leveled in a matter of minutes.

"You still haven't told me what you guys were talking about this morning."

I tried to get her to, but she said it was nothing. I feel her smiling. "We were fighting over who loves you more."

I stiffen at that as she looks up at me, that smile on her lips. "Did you just . . . ?" *Say you love me . . .?*

She shakes her head. "No. He won," she grins, backtracking, "by far."

I chuckle at that, but she did say it.

She loves me.

"I love you too."

I feel her shudder as she leans back into me, looking at our grim surroundings.

Of course, this is when we would finally cop to our feelings.

Great timing.

Mya

THEIR CARS ARE DESTROYED, but Quinn's was okay, so she picked us up and brought us to their home. She and Logan both seem so damn relieved to be together again. I can't imagine Logan's terror during those hours we were stuck in the basement and she was at their house with their kid.

When we get inside, Jase continues trying like crazy to reach Finn. I have a sinking feeling that I can't combat.

"That motherfucker." Jase ends the call and puts his phone back in his pocket and wraps his arms around my waist, his front to my back.

"He's fine," Tommy tries to reassure him. "He's probably still fucking that skanky chick and doesn't even know anything happened."

I smile at Tommy, thinking that's a possibility, but I'm not sure even Finn could ignore the hell that ripped through town. I've never been through an actual tornado. There was a bad storm with microbursts when I was twelve that tore the roof off our apartment building. We were without power for days, but it was nothing like last night.

Jase grumbles and releases me with a quick kiss to the top of my head. "I'm going to go try again." He moves out of the kitchen and heads into the living room.

Tommy and James shake their heads at him, but quickly follow.

Logan takes the baby, giving Quinn a kiss before he leaves the kitchen too. It's just Quinn and me left as she pulls open the refrigerator door. "I guess I should find something to feed everyone."

"I can help." I walk to where she's standing, a bewildered look on her pretty face. "I'm so sorry, Quinn."

Lyrics and Ink was their dream, a beautiful dream they made come true together. And now it's destroyed, completely unrecognizable.

"As long as Finn is alive, we'll be fine."

She closes the fridge and turns to me. My eyes flick to the living room where Jase just disappeared and then back to her. "What if he's not?" I know how close Finn and Jase are, the bile rises in my throat, thinking about him lying somewhere under the rubble.

She takes a deep breath that appears to be painful. "I don't know. I can't think about it."

"I'm so sorry, Quinn," my voice is soft with a sob catching in my throat.

Her eyes are full of concern as she places a hand on my shoulder. "Stop saying that. None of this was your fault."

"Wasn't it?" I wipe a tear from my cheek. "You guys had everything. You got out. You made a beautiful life here. And I came and wrecked it all."

"Don't do that, Mya."

I can't stop the grief coming over me, feeling like a curse. They were all fine.

Her hands hold both my shoulders firmly. "None of this is because of you. Tornados happen."

"What if he's dead, Quinn? They're like brothers. We both know Jase won't handle that."

What if he starts using? I can't fight the feelings taking over me.

"They are, but Finn is fine. I know he is."

I shake my head, knowing no one is safe around me no matter how hard I try to keep them that way. "Your business is destroyed."

"We have insurance. We'll rebuild. We'll do what we have to,

Mya." Her eyes are serious as they hold me hostage. "If there's one thing we know from our upbringing, it's rising up again after tragedy. It's fighting. We keep going."

"I'm tired."

She hugs me, and I let her, tears falling down my face and feeling overwhelmingly exhausted from it all. On the outside, I'm young, but on the inside, years of pain is wearing me out.

"Now this, I can definitely get behind."

I wipe my tears, and Quinn and I both turn toward the voice. I see Finn, standing in the doorway, unharmed and with a smirk on his face. Quinn walks over to him, smacking his arm. "You. Dick. You scared the fuck out of us."

He just grins easily and pulls her into a hug. "I'm fine." He pulls back. "But seriously. Were you and Mya about to have some comforting girl time? Were you about to kiss her and make it all better?"

I roll my eyes, and Quinn punches him in the chest. It's playful, but he still makes an "oomph" sound that makes me smile.

The guys all must hear him because they filter into the kitchen, Jase first. "You motherfucker. You can't use a goddamn phone?"

Finn laughs, pulling him into a quick hug. "It fucking died. Power went out. I'm fine."

"You stayed the night with your hookup?"

He shakes his head, like it's a shame. "Yeah. Kind of had to. Slept in her basement. We were mid-fuck when the sirens started going off."

Tommy gives his shoulder a squeeze. "You kept going didn't you?"

He wags his eyebrows and smirks. "You know it. Why stop?"

I stare at them all, dumbfounded that they're now joking around when only moments ago, most of us were thinking the worst.

Finn grows serious as he eyes Logan and Quinn. "I drove to Lyrics and Ink first. I'm so fucking sorry."

I feel the sorrow in the room now. "We'll figure it out," Quinn says with the same determination she did earlier. "You all lost all of your things."

I didn't even think about the fact that the loft is destroyed, taking most of our worldly possessions.

"They're things." Jase wraps an arm around Finn's neck. "We'll be fine."

James nods in agreement. "The town over is offering discounted hotel rooms." He turns to me. "I booked three rooms. So you can make Jase room with Finn, or have mercy on him and let him stay with you."

I smile, finally letting the relief wash over me.

Finn is safe. We're all okay.

FUCKING FINN, leave it to him to scare the shit out of everyone and be totally fine. I can't express how glad I am that he's okay.

It's been days since the tornado. Tommy, James, Finn, Mya, and I are staying in a shitty hotel in another town while Quinn and Logan get everything figured out.

Logan calls a meeting with Finn, James, and me in Finn's room, and all I can think about is getting back to Mya.

She's been quiet since the tornado. I think it scared her more than she wants to admit.

"So, what's up?" Finn leans back on his elbows and looks at Logan, who looks nervous as fuck.

He runs his fingers through his hair. "Look, guys . . . We've talked to the insurance company, and it's going to take a while to be able to reopen." Not surprising. The tornado tore Nashville apart. "And I talked to Rhys last night . . ."

Finn and I share a quick look, before I say, "Just tell us."

He drops his hand with a sigh. "He needs more tattoo artists. His shop is growing by the day, and all he has is Christian who's still his apprentice."

"You're moving to St. Louis," Finn says it, but we all know it's true.

He nods his head. "Now that we've started our family, I think

Quinn wants to be around Phillip and Gillian." It makes sense. Phillip is Logan's dad, and Gillian is his wife.

I smile. "That's fucking great."

He offers a weak smile. "It is. I think it'll be great. Only a few hours from KC, and Rhys hasn't even given his place a name. Maybe we can talk him into Lyrics and Ink. Who knows. I think Quinn can rebuild the bar next door."

"When do you leave?"

He answers me quickly, "Not just me. You can come too. Start new. It wouldn't be Lyrics and Ink without you guys."

Finn laughs, "Rhys is a dick. No way he wants all three of us too."

"Rhys is smart, he knows he needs help. With us there, business will triple."

"I can't." We look over at James, who's smiling, which feels strange in this somber moment.

"Why?" Logan looks almost hurt.

James stands and places a hand on Logan's shoulder. "Tommy and I started the adoption process. We just found out yesterday. We're getting our kid. We're looking for a house, if there are any left. The kid is five, already in school. We can't change that."

Logan nods his head in understanding and gives him a hug. "I'm so fucking happy for you guys."

"Lucky kid." I grin over at James, who has tears in his eyes. They've wanted this for a while.

Even Finn is smiling. "That's fucking awesome. Shitty timing."

I punch him in the arm. "You staying or going, fucker?"

He shrugs. "You know me. I'm always up for a new adventure. What about you?"

My mind instantly goes to Mya. She doesn't want to live in St. Louis—that, I know for sure. "I don't know."

Finn laughs. "Gotta check with the missus, huh?"

I shrug. "We'll see."

Logan gives a nod. "Okay. We're moving in a week. I know it's fast, but no matter what, you'll all always have a place there."

Afterward, I go into the room I'm sharing with Mya. She's sitting on the bed, flipping through the channels.

"What was that about?"

I take a seat on the bed. "Quinn and Logan are relocating Lyrics and Ink. They're merging with Rhys."

She puts the remote down, her brown eyes on me. "St. Louis?"

I nod. "Yeah. Finn seems ready to go."

I sense the pain she's feeling, and it slices through me. "And you?"

I take her small hand in mine. "I'm not going anywhere without you."

I mean it. I haven't known her long, but I can't survive without her. I don't want to.

"I can't go back there."

I knew that already, and she lays her head on my shoulder, looking so damn lost. "They aren't rebuilding here?"

"No. But I could. I have plenty saved." I could get a loan and start over.

She shakes her head from side to side. "You can't do that for me. They're your family. I won't tear you apart."

"So, I'm supposed to go and leave you here?"

Her shoulder shrugs. "We could make it work. It's not either of us running. It's circumstances."

I turn toward her as she lifts her head and cup her angelic face in my hands. "I won't lose you. I meant what I said, I love you."

She smiles at that, gripping my wrist slightly, holding onto me. "I love you too. But I can't see not letting you go. And I can't go with you."

I don't want to talk about this anymore. I bring my lips to hers and kiss her softly, each second adding to my urgency as I lay her back on the bed.

I'm not letting her go, but we can discuss that later.

Mya

"Are you okay?"

I look across the table at Quinn, who's sipping her coffee and eyeing me with so much concern I think my heart might shatter. I hate how much she cares about me. Our time as friends was really just a blip in time before we grew apart. Still, she cares.

"I'm happy for you and Logan."

"Me too. For two kids who didn't grow up with any real family, it just feels like the right thing now. Phillip and Gillian are amazing. Logan's brother and sister are growing up fast." She smiles sweetly at that, but there's sadness there. "You can come too. You'll always have a place with us. I think Rhys would be relieved."

I cringe, thinking about Rhys and how pained he appeared when I showed up needing help. "I can't go there."

She sighs, taking another sip. I'm sure she already knew that would be my answer. I think Jase knew it to. We spent hours in bed last night, letting our bodies say everything our mouths refused to. I don't want him to leave, but I know he needs to.

I'm sure he doesn't want to leave me behind, but he can't be away from his family.

That's exactly what they are to him.

I look down at my phone that's lighting up with a call. I glance at the caller ID and see a KC number. I silence it and look at Quinn. "I appreciate everything, Quinn."

She shakes her head solemnly. "Don't let your stubbornness win, Mya. I know you love Jase. He definitely loves you. Don't end things."

"I don't have a choice. I don't want the city life. But he needs you guys."

She grabs my hand from across the table. "He needs you."

I shake my head. "We just met."

"You think I didn't need Logan from the get-go?"

"He left you."

He abandoned her and everyone else to move in with his dad. No explanation. "And I thought I was going to die from the pain of that. If you can be with the person you love, you should be. No matter what's thrown your way."

I take a drink of my latte. "I can't."

She squeezes my hand and lets it go. "Do you have enough saved? Do you need anything?"

I shake my head. "You've done more than enough."

"I'll gladly do more. I'm not leaving you here with nothing."

And I know she won't. "I have some money saved. I think I'm going to roll the dice and try to find a small town that has any job open. I just want out, Quinn. I want to feel safe."

I think she's careful with her next words. "Our fate isn't up to us. Danger can find us anywhere."

"For once, I have to feel like I have some sort of control over my destiny. I have to take myself out of the places I fear and do like you said, Quinn. Rise."

She smiles at that and nods her head, looking almost proud. "You will, Mya. You will not only rise through the wreckage that tried to break you. You'll soar."

Grief threatens to take over, thinking about the wreckage of my life.

My mother, Trey, Charity. Now, what's left after the tornado.

Jase is alive and well. I haven't demolished him. But if I leave him, that's exactly what it'll do.

I don't know how to get out of this without doing just that.

Jase

"ARE YOU GOING?" I hold Mya's hand in mine, loving the way it looks and the way it feels. Hers is much smaller, with silky dark skin. Mine is large, calloused with tattoos over the milky white, but they blend perfectly. Her fingers interlock in mine. I don't want to lose this image.

But I don't want it to only be a memory. I need it to be forever.

"I don't want to."

We're lying in bed, both totally naked. But I can't stop staring at our hands as I raise them in the air above us.

"But you should."

"Why?"

"They're your family."

I pull our mingled hands to my chest, laying them over my heart. "And what are you?"

She doesn't miss a beat, but I hear the sadness in her voice. "Just a broken girl you met a few months ago."

"You know you're much more than that to me."

"I want to leave, Jase." I turn to look at her, surprised, but then she clarifies. "The city. I can find a waitress job in a small town near here."

I brush my free hand over her cheek. "I could go too."

A tear wets my hand resting on her face. "You helped me talk about what happened to Trey. I'll never be over that grief, but you helped me begin to cope. I owe you everything, and I can't take you away from your family. But I can't go back there."

"I believe there's more to us."

"I think we're caught up in the moment."

She sits up, pulling her hand from mine, and I move behind her, both of us still seated on the bed. "Don't do this. Don't push me away."

"I'm not." Her head drops. "I can't."

"So, what now?" My hands rest on her bare shoulders.

"You leave tomorrow with them. We say goodbye or see you later or whatever we need to tell ourselves. And we go on." I can't see her face, but I sense she's smiling through tears. "And we rise."

My stomach clenches with intense pain, not wanting this to be over. "We could go higher together."

She turns, her hand sliding over my cheek softly. "Trust me on this, I'll only weigh you down."

"That's not true."

She kisses my lips and stands, dressing quickly. "I'm going to go to dinner with Quinn, sort of a goodbye thing."

I nod, not wanting to take away any time with her friend. I know she needs it. "Will you be back tonight?"

I don't care if I sound desperate. She nods and grabs the door handle, twisting it and leaving me on the bed.

I force myself to get dressed and then go to Finn's room. The fucker is wearing only boxers and has claw marks all over his chest when he pulls the door open. "What time is it?"

"Almost six in the evening." He chuckles, shrugging and taking a seat on the sofa in the hotel. "Your guest still here?"

He shakes his head and leans back. "Nah."

I close the door and take the seat next to him, the weight of my conversation with Mya on my mind. "So, we going tomorrow or what?"

I've avoided a definite answer, and he's given me space. "I don't know."

"What's not to know?"

He knows, but he wants to hear it. "I can't get her out of my head. She won't go."

"All attached." He shakes his head, feigning disappointment.

"Yeah." I smile. "I'm in love with her."

He turns to me, and now he looks genuinely surprised. "Damn."

I nod. "Yeah."

He's smiling as he tilts his head back again. "So, you're going to give everything up for a chick?"

"Nah, I'm going to get everything when I finally convince her she wants me too." I lay my head back too. "Since I met her, all I've wanted is to keep her safe."

He shakes his head. "I never understood you." He's smirking again. "But I suppose you have a lot of your dad in you, man. You want to save her. She has a dark past."

"Don't we all?"

He nods his head. "Yup. She's lucky to have you, but I don't think she's going to make it easy."

Now I'm the one with the smirk across my face. "I hate easy."

"Clearly." He punches my arm. "You've seen darkness. You've seen tragedy. And you still somehow hold on to the light. You're exactly what she needs."

"You're gonna miss me," I joke, trying to lighten the mood.

He swallows tightly as he looks up at the ceiling. "Yeah, I am."

Well fuck, Finn.

I wasn't expecting him to make it all real, but I don't know how I'm going to do this without my best friend by my side.

Still, I know what needs to be done.

For Mya, I'll happily rearrange my entire life.

I DON'T WANT to say goodbye. I hate goodbyes.

But I know I need to let them all go. They paid for the hotel for two more weeks, and Quinn gave me instructions to let her know if I need to stay longer.

Of course, I won't.

I can't take anything else from them.

They're leaving for the airport. The shuttle is here at the hotel and about to leave. Their things are being shipped. It's really happening.

I spent the night wrapped in Jase's body, saying goodbye in our own way, over and over again.

But never saying the words out loud.

Everyone gives each other hugs, Quinn tears up as she hugs Tommy and tells him she'll kick his ass if he doesn't send pictures of his new kid very soon.

He tears up too, and then she moves to me, hugging me so tight I think she'll crack a rib. "You've always been like a little sister to me. Please, please call if you need anything."

I know she doesn't want to leave me here. She's grown up so much since the last time I saw her. "I'll be fine."

She hugs me tighter and then finally releases me. Logan gives me a hug, and then they climb in the shuttle.

Finn surprises me with a big bear hug of his own, whispering into my ear, "Take care of him."

"What?" I pull back, but he's grinning wide as he releases me and hugs his best friend.

"Don't knock her up right away. Make her work for that shit."

Jase pats his back in their manly hug. "Shut the fuck up."

Finn laughs and shoves him away. "I mean it. Although the kid will be fucking gorgeous."

He winks at me and climbs into the shuttle, and I stare at Jase, totally dumbfounded. "What's going on?"

Quinn blows me a kiss, her face telling of her knowledge. The shuttle pulls away, and I turn to Jase, ignoring Tommy and James's gigantic smiles.

"What are you doing? Why aren't you leaving?"

He takes my hand in his. "I'm not going."

I look behind him at Tommy and James. "Are you going to rebuild with them?"

He shakes his head, and Tommy snickers. "No. I'm going with you. We're going to start our future." He wraps his strong arms around me. "I'm going to marry you as soon as you let me. And I'm going to knock you up as soon as you're ready. And no matter what, I'm not letting you go. It was never an option."

I shake my head, but I don't push his body away. "You're insane."

"I talked to Spencer last night. He's moving to St. Louis when he turns eighteen to work with Rhys. So, he'll be okay. His birthday is soon."

"I can't go to St. Louis."

He chuckles, cupping my face in his hands and tipping my face up. "I've been paying attention, woman. I get that."

"So, what are we doing?"

"There's a town about an hour south of here. Population 823. They have this plot of land that's perfect for us. A place in town we can rent while they build our house and cheap real estate in their downtown."

I swallow, looking into his eyes. "That's a lot of investment."

"I'm for it. I'm ready. We'll live out in the country. I don't want farm animals, but if you do, we can figure that out . . ."

I laugh and shake my head. "No. Cows freak me out."

He laughs at that. "We'll build a house, and we'll have a quiet, safe life."

"We can't hide from tornados."

He smiles and releases my face but hugs me to him. "We'll build a basement."

I sigh into him. Safe. That all sounds safe for the first time in my life. It's my dream.

"You'll be bored."

Again he laughs and pulls back enough to look down into my eyes. "Yeah, there's no fucking way life with you could ever be boring. And running our own businesses, we'll be busy."

"Businesses?"

Tommy and James now join us. James is smiling in my direction. "Yeah, you have some investors already. And soon, they'll be more than silent partners."

"What the hell are you talking about?" My eyebrow arches in question.

Jase answers, "Tommy and James are going to invest in our tavern."

I turn to him, shocked. "Tavern? You're a tattoo artist."

"And hopefully, I can open a small shop. But for a while, the tavern is already established, and the owner is looking to sell and retire. It's perfect."

I turn to Tommy. "You'll be joining us?"

My heart squeezes with anticipation because I want them to. In the short time I've been here, they've become my family. "Yeah. After we get acquainted with our son and make sure the schools there will be adequate."

I nod. "Of course."

Tommy shrugs. "I'm anxious to live in a safe small town too. Although . . ." he looks at his husband. "they might not be ready for us."

"Fuck their ready," I say with more confidence than I feel. I hadn't thought about the small-town aspect, that they might not be as welcoming to a Black woman or a Black man with an Hispanic husband. I feel an uncomfortable fear slide through me, but Jase grips my shoulders.

"It's a great place. It is. I promise. And if you hate it, or you don't feel safe, we can move, but it's pretty diverse. No serious crimes in years. They don't seem to have any violence issues."

"Sounds like heaven."

"It will be."

He's always so damn sure of everything. "Do you really have enough for this?"

"I have enough saved for a down payment, especially with our partners here." He smiles over at Tommy and James and then looks at me. "Why? Are you a gold digger?"

"Don't make me stab you."

He chuckles, but I'm not sure I can do this.

"You've saved your whole life for that money. You love to save people and take care of them. This is just you saving me."

"There's nothing wrong with being rescued, Mya. Have faith. You're what I want."

"Why are you doing this?"

"Because I love you."

"I love you too."

He smiles, pressing a kiss to my lips. "I know. Now let's go back to our room and get started on our plan. After we fuck, of course."

I roll my eyes and shove him playfully away from me. "So damn romantic."

For once though, I'm going with it. I'm going to put myself first and go after what I want.

Because I want Jase.

6 months later

"SING FOR ME." It's a quiet command that sends shivers through me.

"Bossy." Jase grins at me, his smile bright and beautiful. He flips the sign on our tavern to "Closed" and locks the door.

"It's just us."

The sale of this place happened surprisingly fast. Tommy and James are moving here in a month, and their son, Milo, couldn't be happier. He talks about it every time we FaceTime with them or they visit.

The town is small, but it's warm. Everyone seems to know each other, which was intimidating at first. But it was like they adopted us right away, bringing us pies and casseroles and welcoming us to town.

One thing we added to the small tavern that had three booths, two tables, a jukebox and a pool table, was a stage. A stage with one microphone in the center. Every Friday, we have a live show featuring different bands and singers who sign up.

It's been soothing to my soul. I've grown to love this tavern and its patrons. I can't wait for James and Jase to open their tattoo parlor. I know he misses it, even if he seems to enjoy working here.

And we both enjoy the live music and seeing people dancing in the middle of the small tavern.

Still, Jase wants me up there. And how can I deny my husband of that?

A simple ceremony two months ago has bound us together forever. Quinn, Logan, and Finn flew in. Rhys surprised me by showing up with his wife. And so did Sean.

A piece of me ached to not have Charity there even if I knew that was next to impossible. I pray she's alive, but after this long . . . the odds aren't great.

There will always be some guilt tied to her. I wish I could have done more. I wish she would have reached out.

I know I need to let that go.

I walk up onto the stage and grip the metal microphone with my hands.

I stare out at him. Free, freer than I've ever felt in my life.

He isn't an addict, but he still goes to meetings. He found one here at the local church. He found a couple of people to sponsor too. He's a healer whether he realizes it or not.

I sing. And I release my pain.

Some of it will always stay with me, but I've learned to have faith. To trust that there's still good in the world.

Who knows? Maybe someday there'll be justice for my little brother. Or his story will spark change. Maybe guilt will eat his killer alive, and he'll confess to his crimes.

Sometimes the hope of all of that is stifling and painful. But I know one thing, Jase is good.

And he's mine.

My mother never had that. She never brought a good man around. I never saw any of my friends with good parents. I didn't know good existed. I saw small flashes but was never immersed in it until I met him.

And he looks at me, like *I'm* the good. Like I bring him hope. Why or how I have no idea, but I never want to stop being that for him.

When I finish the song, he's on me like a flash, his mouth devouring mine.

"My voice really does get you hot, huh?"

"Fuck yeah." He starts to strip me, and I do the same, my hands dragging over his muscular arms.

"I love you."

"I love you."

"Haven't changed your mind?"

His fingers sweep over my hardened nipples through my bra. "Hell no."

We lie down on the stage, and he enters me at an achingly slow pace, making me groan with need. "I'll never change my mind when it comes to you, Mya. You're what I wanted from the day I saw you."

"I never believed love could happen like that."

"It does. It hit me hard."

I smile. "I don't think I ever had a chance of really leaving you behind once I had you."

He smiles and pushes all the way inside me.

"We're going to be happy, Mya. We're going to make a ton of tiny little humans, and we're going to make sure they're good. We're going to make the world better by just being together."

"That seems a little egomaniacal."

He pulls back and then thrusts inside me. "I have a large *ego*."

I roll my eyes but bite my bottom lip as he fills me. "Then let's get this going already."

He laughs at that but increases his pace. I'm eager to feel him release deep inside me. I want this next step with him. I went off birth control the day we got married. I didn't think I'd ever want to bring babies into this dark world. But that was before Jase.

Before he showed me this part of the world. The good part, full of light and hope.

I'm forever grateful to this man for that.

Jase

Almost eight months later

"Oh my God, why can't they leave me alone?" My *very* pregnant wife groans when her phone starts to ring on the table next to our bed.

"Ignore it." I kiss her cheek, and the phone stops. But then, it immediately rings again.

Okay, that's enough. I grab her phone and answer it before she can object. "What?"

"Mm . . .Mya? Is Mya there?" A shaky voice comes over the line, and I know this isn't a reporter.

"This is her husband."

"Oh . . ." she sounds surprised, "um . . . This is Charity . . . I . . ."

Charity. That Charity? I mouth her name to Mya. She struggles to sit up, her pregnant belly making it hard, and I help her as she takes the phone.

"Charity? What's wrong?"

Mya's eyes are full of tears as she listens and chokes on a sob.

"Oh my God. Are you okay?"

I hold my breath in my lungs as I wait. Mya is almost nine months pregnant. We have a house. Our business is doing well.

I know she has a phobia that once things are going well, something will destroy it.

Tears slide down her cheeks as she shakes her head. "I'm so sorry, Charity. I would gladly come and get you, but . . ." her eyes flick to mine, "I don't think I can fly. I'm pregnant. Really, pregnant."

"What's going on?"

She looks at me, her eyes hopeless. "She's in the hospital in Kansas City."

I immediately pull out my phone, needing to fix this.

"Yeah. I know. A lot has changed. But still . . . I'd be there for you in a heartbeat. I live in Tennessee now."

I call Finn, and he answers on the second ring, "What the fuck? You realize it's midnight, and my cock is buried in—"

"Stop," I silence him. "I'm sorry, but I need a favor."

Mya's eyes dart to me. "Hang on, Charity."

"What's wrong?" I hear the concern in Finn's voice.

"Mya's friend Charity is in the hospital. She needs someone to pick her up."

"Are you fucking kidding me?"

"Do I sound like I'm kidding. I'm sorry I interrupted, but I need you to pull out and go help her."

Mya's eyes widen, and I shake my head, winking at her.

"Fuck. Fine. Which hospital."

I turn to Mya. "What hospital."

She speaks into the phone, "Which hospital? We have a friend who can help." Silence and deep concern. "No, Charity. It's no problem. No, please don't hang up." Her voice sounds desperate and turns into a shrill cry as she lowers her phone, the tears flowing. "She said she didn't know I was pregnant or she never would have called. She wouldn't tell me which hospital."

My heart aches for my beautiful wife, and I know I'm going to owe Finn huge. "She wouldn't say what hospital, but it's in Kansas City."

I can hear him dressing and smile when I hear keys jingle. "You're saying you want me to drive three fucking hours to Kansas City and go to, what, twenty fucking hospitals and ask for Mya's friend?"

"Charity."

"Fuck."

Mya starts to get out of bed, and I know this stubborn woman has it in her head that she's going to Kansas City. I take her hand in mine and shake my head. "Finn, I need your help. Mya is too pregnant, and by the time I can get a flight there or drive, Charity will probably be gone."

"I'm going, asshole. But fuck."

I grin and then let out a relieved breath. "He's going."

Mya holds her hand out for my phone, and I give it to her. "Finn?" She rolls her eyes. "Listen to me. She's in trouble. She wouldn't give me many details, but she said they won't let her leave unless someone signs her out. I don't know why she wouldn't call her brother, Christian, but she's been gone for so long . . ." She starts to cry, and I can't imagine Finn will handle that well. She laughs and wipes her tears. "Asshole."

I growl, not wanting to know what my best friend said.

"Thank you for this. Please keep her safe."

She hands the phone back to me. "Hey."

"Hey. Look, I kicked the chick out, and I'm in my car. Don't let her get her hopes up, man. This sounds like a fucking long shot."

"I know." I smile sadly at Mya. "Try. Please. I'll owe you one."

"You'll owe me a shit ton."

I smile because I know it's not really true. Finn's my brother.

We hang up, and I hug Mya's body to me, kissing the top of her head. "It's going to be okay."

She shakes her head. "It was her calling me. All this time, I thought she was dead or hated me, but she was reaching out for help."

This guilt is going to eat her alive.

"Mya, she never left a message. You had no way of knowing."

She wipes at her tears, and I hold her closer. "He has to find her. She's afraid. I heard the terror in her voice. She's in trouble, Jase."

"It's okay. Finn will find her." I turn her face to look at me and kiss her softly. "I love you. He loves you. And he'll find her."

She nods her head, holding back her tears as she rests it on my shoulder.

It may be a longshot, but one thing is for sure . . .

Finn doesn't give up easily.

The End

NOTE FROM THE AUTHOR

I really hope you enjoyed Jase and Mya's story. I absolutely love them and although this story was different for me I knew I wanted to tell it. Mya's story is tragic, and it happens all too often. I wanted this series to be about the forgotten kids. The ones who have to raise themselves and sometimes their siblings too.

As a mother, it's hard for me to stomach that there are kids who aren't taken care of and cherished. If I think about it too often, it cripples me. I want all kids to be treated as if they are precious because they are. I want everyone to feel safe in their homes as well as out in the world. I believe it starts with individuals, with one act of kindness.

And I want people to have hope. I'll never stop believing there is good in this world. I know all about the bad but want the good to win. I'll never stop that fight, and I want to encourage everyone else to do the same.

Don't give up. Always fight for what's right. Nothing is hopeless. I truly believe we can do better. Be kind and spread the kindness.

Thank you so much to all of my friends and family who are the good in my life, who don't let me give up. Thank you to Harper and Lyla for lighting a fire in me when I was in my mid-twenties, for making me a mom hell-bent on making sure you grow up in a better world.

Thank you to my husband, who grounds me when I feel like I can't take the bad, who kisses my forehead and tells me I'm amazing and to "chill out." I love you forever and always.

Thank you, Jeanna, for your love and support. You're way stronger than you think, and you deserve only good things. Thank you, Emma, for always being there to listen when I'm having a terrible day. Ari, thank you for your gross/amazing pep talks and keeping me going when I feel like I'm not good enough. Thank you, Elle, for being you, for being passionate about the world becoming better even when you feel hopeless. I swear to you, you're making a difference. Every bit of good matters. Don't let hate and bad win.

Thank you to Dena for putting up with me. Seriously. Thank you for being my editor and friend. Elizabeth and Veronique, thank you so much for making my books pretty.

Thank you to the Novelties for your fierce support and loyalty. Man, I love you all so much!

Finally, to my parents, thank you. It's hard to put into words how grateful I am for you. You always kept going. Even when things seemed tragic and impossibly difficult, you showed me how to rise. You told me I could soar. I love you both with all my heart.

Thank you all for reading! Don't lose hope!

Made in the USA
Coppell, TX
26 December 2021